WISHFUL WITNESS

THE WISHING TREE BOOK 13

TONYA KAPPES

PRAISE FOR TONYA KAPPES

★★★★★ "Tonya is the modern day Agatha Christie with a southern flair!" Amazon Review

★★★★★ "Tonya's books are just so good!! I can't wait until the next one is out. I'm waiting for the next Mae West to come out!! I love camping and this series makes me want to go to the Daniele Boon National Forest!! Right now I'm reading Kenni Lowry series! Tonya is awesome!" Raelene Shaw Cowley, Goodreads Review

★★★★★ "The characters in Tonya Kappes's Cozy Mystery books become like friends. Reading the the different series of books is like catching up with long-time friends. Each time a new one comes out is like a dinner of comfort food." Melody Pugh Wortmann, Bookbub Reviewer

★★★★★ "I love reading Tonya's books because they are fun! When I grab a glass of sweet ice tea and sit down with the the gang we're going to have a great time." Quincie Ellis, Amazon Reviewer

\

Wishful Witness
By
Tonya Kappes

Published in the United States by Tonya Kappes Books
Printed in the United States of America

Cover by Elizabeth Mackey Graphic Design
Editing by Red Adept Publishing

For Cheryl Standafer. Her unwavering kindness she shows so many along her path. I am forever grateful for her friendship and unconditional spirit love that radiates within her.

ZONING, ZEALOTS, & ZIPLINES
HAMMOCKS, HANDGUNS, & HEARSAY

Kenni Lowry Mystery Series
FIXIN' TO DIE
SOUTHERN FRIED
AX TO GRIND
SIX FEET UNDER
DEAD AS A DOORNAIL
TANGLED UP IN TINSEL
DIGGIN' UP DIRT
BLOWIN' UP A MURDER

Killer Coffee Mystery Series
SCENE OF THE GRIND
MOCHA AND MURDER
FRESHLY GROUND MURDER
COLD BLOODED BREW
DECAFFEINATED SCANDAL
A KILLER LATTE
HOLIDAY ROAST MORTEM
DEAD TO THE LAST DROP
A CHARMING BLEND NOVELLA (CROSSOVER WITH MAGICAL
CURES MYSTERY)
FROTHY FOUL PLAY
SPOONFUL OF MURDER
BARISTA BUMP-OFF
CAPPUCCINO CRIMINAL

Holiday Cozy Mystery
FOUR LEAF FELONY
MOTHER'S DAY MURDER
A HALLOWEEN HOMICIDE
NEW YEAR NUISANCE

CHOCOLATE BUNNY BETRAYAL
APRIL FOOL'S ALIBI
FATHER'S DAY MURDER
THANKSGIVING TREACHERY
SANTA CLAUSE SURPRISE

Mail Carrier Cozy Mystery
STAMPED OUT
ADDRESS FOR MURDER
ALL SHE WROTE
RETURN TO SENDER
FIRST CLASS KILLER
POST MORTEM
DEADLY DELIVERY
RED LETTER SLAY

Magical Cures Mystery Series
A CHARMING CRIME
A CHARMING CURE
A CHARMING POTION (novella)
A CHARMING WISH
A CHARMING SPELL
A CHARMING MAGIC
A CHARMING SECRET
A CHARMING CHRISTMAS (novella)
A CHARMING FATALITY
A CHARMING DEATH (novella)
A CHARMING GHOST
A CHARMING HEX
A CHARMING VOODOO
A CHARMING CORPSE
A CHARMING MISFORTUNE
A CHARMING BLEND (CROSSOVER WITH A KILLER COFFEE
COZY)

A CHARMING DECEPTION

A Southern Magical Bakery Cozy Mystery Serial
A SOUTHERN MAGICAL BAKERY

A Ghostly Southern Mystery Series
A GHOSTLY UNDERTAKING
A GHOSTLY GRAVE
A GHOSTLY DEMISE
A GHOSTLY MURDER
A GHOSTLY REUNION
A GHOSTLY MORTALITY
A GHOSTLY SECRET
A GHOSTLY SUSPECT

A Southern Cake Baker Series
(WRITTEN UNDER MAYEE BELL)
CAKE AND PUNISHMENT
BATTER OFF DEAD

Spies and Spells Mystery Series
SPIES AND SPELLS
BETTING OFF DEAD
GET WITCH or DIE TRYING

A Laurel London Mystery Series
CHECKERED CRIME
CHECKERED PAST
CHECKERED THIEF

A Divorced Diva Beading Mystery Series
A BEAD OF DOUBT SHORT STORY
STRUNG OUT TO DIE
CRIMPED TO DEATH

CHAPTER 1

There was always so much to do in the morning I rarely took the time to enjoy the sunrise. But on this particular morning, the cotton-candy pink, baby blue, and slight tinge of red blanketed the sky over Linden Falls, letting off a warm glow through the windows of the Stitchin' Post, my yarn shop.

I'd been sitting on the floor, putting out the new fall line of yarns in the baskets, when I'd noticed the early morning light, and for a second—like one of those intuitive moments—I felt a tug to go and enjoy this moment of peace before what was going to be a very long and busy day.

Instead of worrying with the yarn, I followed my gut and got up, picking up my coffee mug from the counter on my way over to the display window, which just so happened to have the best view of Town Square and the Wishing Tree, our town's most popular attraction.

Little slips of paper tied to the tree flittered as a fall breeze blew across the grassy green area. Each one gave hope to one day having their wish fulfilled when, with anxious hearts, individuals wrote out their wish and tied it to one of the Wishing Tree's branches.

My heart was full just thinking about all the good the tree had done for so many people. Me included.

Someone had tied a wish on the tree, from a local child, to turn the local SPCA into a no-kill animal shelter, and Friends for Life was birthed. If it weren't for the owners coming into the Stitchin' Post to see if they could buy some blankets for the animals in the shelter as they waited for their furever home, I wouldn't've started my knitting group, where we met weekly to knit blankets for the animals for free.

Not only did the wish grant me a set of new friends that I called on during all times of my life, but it gave me a companion.

Tilly.

Tilly was my tortoiseshell cat, who literally adopted me the day I walked into Friends for Life with the knitting club's set of donated blankets.

Just that one wish gave me an entirely new life, and it wasn't even one I'd put on the tree.

The memory made me smile as I drank my coffee and let the morning rays shine a spotlight on the wishes. Out of the corner of my eye, I saw something move.

My eyes shifted, and I squinted into the dawn, where I tried to make out who on earth was in the town square so early. After all, I was the only person I knew who got to their shop even before Doc's Fountains, the local café that now opened early due to their trendy coffees being so popular, began daily business.

The sun was moving higher into the sky and giving more and more light to the downtown area, including the square, bringing the silhouette I'd been following into full view.

"Max?" I questioned the man who'd recently bought the King Building across the square and turned it into what he called an artisan market.

A fancy name for a flea market, if you asked me. Or at least that's what Calvin, the reporter for the *Linden Falls Gazette*, had made it sound like after he'd come in here to get some local snapshots to fill up the paper. Calvin had his pulse on everything and everyone in Linden Falls. He sure did have the Linden Falls knitters' yarn all in a tangle after he told us about what Max and Janie were doing with the historical building.

From what I recalled—though it was early this morning, and I was only on my first cup of coffee until Crooked Porch Café opened—Calvin had mentioned how Janie questioned her husband.

"We already have a farmers market where a lot of people sell their wares," Calvin repeated what he'd heard Janie say.

To which Max replied, "This is going to be more than that. I plan to build it as a permanent venue for events. Part of it will have booths for artists to display their work. Anything from paintings to poetry to quilts. Anything that takes creative talent. The other part of the building will be rented out for various fairs and visiting craft shows. Possibly even author events, seeing how Vermont is known as a writer's retreat."

Like the rest of the knitting club, I wasn't sure how something like that would go over here in Linden Falls since Janie was right. There was already a weekly farmers market right there under the Wishing Tree.

But neither Max nor Janie asked for my opinion, though they did offer me a booth to sell things from my shop. I had politely declined for two reasons.

One, I owned my own shop, and the rent there was already steep. Again, the Stitchin' Post had the best views of downtown, and that included the King Building. Two, they were asking for a crazy fee to have a booth there, and it didn't make sense to have a booth and a shop.

"What are you doing?" I mumbled to myself as I watched as Max reached up to read one of the wishes on a low-hanging branch before he snatched it off. Then he repeated the same action a few more times.

A flicker of light caught my eye, and I looked away from Max toward the Crooked Porch Café. I glanced at my watch because I knew they came in around six a.m. to get ready for the breakfast rush around seven. This was my signal to get the rest of my morning shop routine done so I could open at eight a.m. Then I'd walk across the square to the café to pick up my daily breakfast order when they opened.

When I turned back to the Wishing Tree and Max's shenanigans, he was gone, and my curious side kicked into full gear.

"Odd," I thought and headed back to the shipment of new fall yarns I'd ordered a couple of months ago to make sure I had enough in stock for the "Mocha Medley" project I'd promised would be an easy project for the beginning knitter.

At least that's what the large chalkboard sign I'd propped up in the display window announced, with a gorgeous throw on display next to it.

I'd gotten a lot of people to sign up for the class. Not only was it a beginner class, but the throw would make an excellent Christmas gift for a man or a woman.

Right now, during the fall months, was prime time for early Christmas shoppers to start getting gifts, and a handmade gift as lovely as a knitted blanket was not only personal, but loving. The next couple months beginner's knitting class was just the right timing for the holiday.

The new yarn had to be put out this morning because the new class started tonight, which was going to make for a very long day.

By the time I'd gotten the yarns in the baskets and moved them around to make the perfect display, it was time for me to go grab my coffee and breakfast at the Crooked Porch Café.

I'd completely forgotten about seeing Max plucking off a few wishes until I stepped outside the shop and locked it, only to turn around and face the tree.

It was odd, due to the fact I'd never heard of Max granting anything but money in his pocket. Though it was gossip, I'd still never seen the man do anything charitable.

"Good morning, Cheryl," Nicole greeted me from behind the counter at the café as soon as the bell over the door dinged my arrival. "Your breakfast is right over there."

She pointed to the end of the counter, where my breakfast biscuit sandwich and large to-go cup of coffee were sitting. There was a sun drawn on the paper sack with my name scribbled above it.

"Thanks!" I called to her. She was at the opposite end of the diner, going from table to table filling up the saltshakers. "How long have you been here?"

"Just about forty minutes, or maybe longer." She looked up and shrugged. "Why?"

"I was curious to see if you saw someone hanging around the Wishing Tree this morning." I had a knack for beating around the bush to get people to talk. That's what made the Linden Falls Knitters Club so much fun.

The gossip.

"No. You didn't see who it was?" Her brows pinched.

"Nah. Too dark." I was careful not to tell gossip, just listen. If it got around town the owner of the knitting shop gossiped, I'd never have a customer. But when word around town talked about how much fun it was to sit and gab at the Stitchin' Post during the Linden Falls Knitters Club, that was a whole different story. In reality, it was just a proper way to tell people, *"You should join the knitting club. You hear all sorts of gossip."*

"Let me know if you hear anything about someone roaming around. You know, if something happened to a shop or to someone, we'd need to tell Hector." I picked up my bag as I referred to Hector Norton, Linden Falls Chief of Police.

"Yeah. Scary." Her voice trailed off, and she looked out toward the tree. "I'll keep my ears peeled."

"Don't forget knitting club is tonight. Beginner's class. Hope to see you there," I called over my shoulder before I headed out the door.

Nicole wasn't in the knitting club, nor did she ever express interest. I didn't even know her history or who her friends were. I just knew her from picking up my morning coffee and breakfast for the last few years and having these quick five-minute conversations with her. It wouldn't hurt to offer a friendly invite to join.

Goose bumps ran along my spine and landed across my arms when I passed by the Wishing Tree. I wrapped my knitted cashmere shawl around my neck a little tighter and picked up my speed.

I couldn't get in the shop quick enough.

CHAPTER 2

*M*ost of the day was spent getting the online shop orders packaged and ready to ship. A perk to having my own shop was time. There was plenty of time for me to sit behind the counter when a class wasn't going on and knit my day away.

The bright-orange colorful room was always inviting for knitters to come in and cheerfully sit with a pair of needles in their hands. No matter what the weather, it was always sparkly in the Stitchin' Post.

It made it easy for me to happily make products to sell and feature in my online shop that was maintained by my boyfriend, Vance Stratton. Vance was a web designer for a large firm, and I was lucky to be his first guinea pig when he'd gone out on his own. To say I had the latest and greatest online shop was an understatement. Since Vance had gone full-time with his own web design company, my sales have tripled. Which meant every single free minute I had during the day, I was making new products to add to the website.

I also took special orders, and right now cardigans and shawls were hot ticket items. Today was the day to get some of those packaged and out the door, which was tedious but made the day fly by without me even realizing the time when I looked up and Sharon Bradford, my best friend, came waltzing through the door with her Stitchin' Post knitting bag dangling off her shoulder.

"Oh no." I jerked up and looked at the clock from the workstation behind my counter. It was a place I could package orders and keep an eye on the shop. The classes were held in a dedicated room in the back of the shop, and I closed the shop during class time. "Is it already time for class?"

"No. How ya doing, Sharon?" she asked with snark. "Oh, I'm fine. I was at work today, and Truman asked me out. That's all."

"Shut up!" I squealed and put the packaging tape down so I could run around the counter and give her a huge hug for her accomplishment of getting the new guy in her architecture office to notice her.

"I couldn't wait to tell you, so I thought I'd come a little early, grab you, head over to the King Building to get a look around since it is opening day." Sharon was a devious one, and I loved her all the more for it. "I can tell you all about Truman so then we can gossip about it at class."

Sharon was always up for some fun, and if it weren't for her, you'd think I was a recluse instead of a typical twenty-eight-year-old.

"You never know." She picked up one of the shawls I was about to put into the envelope for the mailman to pick up that afternoon. "You might change your mind and open a booth there."

"That wouldn't help my bottom line. The rent here is already steep, and I can't do both. Besides, it's worldly out there. And I just so happen to love being in here with my thoughts." This was the one thing Sharon had always tried to change in me since the day we met in college, not too far from here.

"Good, because what Max and Janie did to that place is a crime." Sharon and her other architecture friends were up front and center when the town held a vote on whether or not to let Max purchase it from the town.

It was one of the oldest buildings in town, and the design was classic or something, according to Sharon.

It was Sharon who begged me to come with her when she'd gotten the architect job. Since I couldn't imagine life without my best friend, and I didn't have a teaching job offer, I decided to take the plunge.

Granted, I never applied to any teaching jobs, and honestly, sitting around my grandmother's house, watching her knit, then her teaching, was a much better education than any college degree. When I told my parents I wanted to move to Linden Falls, even farther away from my hometown, they were so excited to think about me using my education to help children. When I told them I wanted to open a shop in Linden Falls, well, they nearly lost their marbles.

Like all things, they eventually came around. Not in person. No. They'd never visited my shop or even Linden Falls, but they accepted I was going to forge my own path, to which they told me I had to pay off my student loans without any of their help.

"It's what adults do after they get a job. Now that you've decided to knit all day, that is your job," was pretty much how they worded it.

"Earth to Cheryl." Sharon singsonged into the air, waving a knitting needle at me. "Let's go. I'm starving."

"Fine. Let me package this last one up." I carefully folded the shawl and wrapped it in some tissue paper before sealing it with a cute sticker with the logo of the shop on it. "Presentation is everything."

"Uh-huh." Sharon hummed, not caring a bit about what the package looked like. I saw her rip into them firsthand, and a little bit of my shop-owner heart died every time she did. "Let's go."

She stood at the shop door with the small basket I left outside for the mailman to take mail and leave mail. Linden Falls wasn't any sort of crime-ridden neighborhood. In fact, I could leave the shop door unlocked all the time, and nothing would ever get stolen.

I likened it to those feel-good romance movies you see on television. The yucky, make-you-sick kinda shows. Linden Falls was truly like one of those shows. And I'd embraced the yucky, sick-to-my-stomach romances here along with all the nice folks in town.

But that didn't mean there wasn't any gossip, and if one thing was for sure, the King Building had been at the center of gossip at the Linden Falls Knitters Club.

Plus I was hungry. Getting something to eat was probably the best thing to do before I tried to teach new knitters how to properly lay a ball of yarn in their lap so the thread unraveled easily while knitting.

It was basic things I was going to be teaching tonight, and with the help of the experienced knitters in the club, I would surely have some assistance.

"Tell me all about Truman, and don't leave out a single detail." I had no idea why I said the last thing because that was what Sharon was good at. Make it *great* at. The details.

"You know, I went into work this morning wearing this." She gestured to the pants and cardigan I'd made for her, which pleased me to no end that she had it on. "And, of all days, he came into my office to see if I would like a coffee because he'd gotten enough for everyone in the office."

I'd planned on listening intently to her, but as we walked through the park, the closer we got to the Wishing Tree, which brought back all the memories from this morning. Almost foggy, now that I'd had my coffee and moved on with the day, but the same goose bumps I'd felt this morning crawled right back into my memory.

"Great!" Sharon threw her hands up in the air. "Don't tell me you're coming down with something. Are you getting the fall allergies? You spend all your extra money on allergy medication to not get a sinus infection, and the way you just shivered is the exact same way you shiver right before you come down with something. Which means I could get something."

Sharon brought me out of my head.

"What?" I asked, blinking a few times.

"You." She threw her palm on my forehead. "You don't feel warm."

"I'm fine," I assured her. "I'm not getting sick. Just a cold breeze."

There wasn't any sense in telling her about seeing Max removing the wishes off the tree. She already had a beef with the man over the King Building.

"Look at that." Sharon's face lit up with glee. She pointed to a group of three people holding up signs in protest of the building. "I love it. Good for them."

"What on earth are they protesting?" I tried to read the sign, but we were still too far away, plus they were flailing around, pumping them in the air with the beat of their voices. It was hard to read.

Sharon's stomach must've done a flip-flop and forgotten it was hungry because she made a beeline over to the protest line.

"Yes!" Sharon hollered out and clapped as Zeke Turner, an old farmer, walked by, pumping his homemade sign in the air.

"What on earth is going on?" I asked Zeke as he approached us.

"Max and Janie are taking food right out of our mouths." His crooked finger pointed to the building. "We had a perfectly great place for the farmers market there. The fee was reasonable, and everyone was happy. Then that shmuck buys up the old King Building and not only triples the price, but we have to have certain signs. All matching each other."

Sharon had taken Zeke's sign and took his place in the three-person protest while he stood there talking to me.

"Me and Darlene can't afford those prices. Neither can Andrea. Right, Andrea?" he asked Andrea Jones when she walked past us.

"That's right. We rely on our gardens and the goods we grow to sell at the market so we can live during the brutal Vermont winter months. With these prices, we'd have to make our gardens at least four times as big." She pumped her sign and continued to walk. "That means we have to buy more seeds, soil, and tools. It ain't free!" She hollered for the sake of hollering even though I could hear her perfectly.

By the time Zeke had told me all about their protest and how the three of them, him, Andrea, and Martin Rye, had come up with a plan about how they were going to continue to protest until the next town meeting, which was at least a month away, a crowd had gathered around to see what all the commotion was about.

"Excuse me, excuse me." Mayor O'Brien pushed his way up to the front of the crowd and approached the three protesters and Sharon.

"What is going on here? I got a call from Hector Norton saying there was a disturbance outside of the King Building. He thought I'd be able to come over here and straighten it out before they came down here to arrest someone."

"We aren't doing anything illegal." Zeke butted his chest up to Mayor O'Brien. "We are using our freedom as law-abiding citizens to point out how Max is a criminal by overcharging the price of having a booth in the *Artisan Market*." The sarcasm in Zeke's voice made everyone snicker.

"Max can do what he wants. He does own the building now, and if you don't like it, you don't have to participate."

"We can't participate." Andrea glared at Mayor O'Brien. "None of us can afford the booth price, not to mention all the added expenses." She rambled them off.

"We came to the meetings, and no one wanted to listen to us. All you heard was 'booths' and 'rent' and 'what tourists will love.' Not the good citizens of Linden Falls." Martin didn't stop flailing his sign in the air. "And we are going to protest to let all those tourists and our friends know what this man has done."

Sharon had given Zeke his sign back.

"Let's go. I'm hungry." She tugged on my sleeve. Now that she had stirred the pot, she wanted to get out before it started to boil, and by the volume of the group, it was going to get uglier before it got better. "It's a shame what Max and Janie have done, if what Zeke says is true."

"Calvin Phelps told me all about it, but I never mentioned it because it was just hearsay. But from the looks of it, Max has gone full force." I stopped talking once we walked inside the building and noticed what Max had talked about was brought to life.

Inside of the old building was exactly what he'd promised. The open area had several tables set up along each side with various vendors who were apparently willing to pay the fee to be there.

It did look nice with all the uniform white tablecloths and signs posted behind them of who they were and what they sold. It was all very pretty, but was it really necessary?

"I'm beginning to see Zeke's point." I hated to even say it because Sharon started off on that tangent.

"I know. The farmers market is just that." She twisted toward me and threw up her hands. "A farmers market. With all the little woven baskets filled with berries, vegetables, and the stacked ears of corn, right?"

"Yeah." I walked up to Nick Sutton's table. "Hey, Nick."

"Cheryl!" He seemed a little too happy to see me. "Are you getting excited for the new knitting class tonight?"

"I am." I was taken aback that he even knew about the class.

"Are you coming, Nick?" Sharon asked with some trepidation. "I mean, knitting is for everyone." She ran her hand down her cardigan. "Cheryl made this. Isn't it gorgeous?"

"I walked by this morning and saw the sign in the window. That's all." Nick blushed. "Anyways, I've got some awesome butter beans. The kind you like, right over there." He pointed me to the other side of his booth.

"Wow." I clamped my mouth shut when I noticed the prices of his butter beans had tripled.

"Yeah. They look great this season, right?" He picked up two small baskets, one in each hand. "Two today?"

"I'm going to pass today." I smiled and turned around to keep moving through the building so I could get out of there.

"What?" He got my attention. "You aren't going to buy them?"

"I'm sorry, Nick, but they are a little out of my budget." I hated to be honest with him. "I'm not sure why they tripled since last week, and I do love them, but I simply can't afford them."

"You should be ashamed of yourself, Nick Sutton." Sharon jerked my arm and twisted me around to where we'd come from. "We can buy frozen butter beans from the grocery store for far less than what you were even selling them for last week." She tugged me to walk with her. "Besides, Cheryl was only being nice to you by buying them anyways for the last couple of years. You two being on the local small business board and all."

Over my shoulder, I looked back at him and gave him a weak smile.

He simply glared.

The goose bumps reappeared, only this time they covered my entire body.

CHAPTER 3

"It was highway robbery. That's what that was." Sharon rocked back and forth in the rocker, going to town on the blanket for the Friends for Life. She couldn't wait until all the new students had taken their yarns and made the twelve balls they needed for the fifty-by-sixty-inch blanket the class was making by using the shop's swift ball winder I kept for the students.

Poor girl had been working on that particular blanket all summer long, and here we were in the middle of fall. The rate she was going, one stitch for class, the blanket would be ready by this time next year.

"The price Nick Sutton is asking for butter beans got me all riled up." The yarn fell from her needles as she pointed them in the air. "I'm glad to see the protesters too."

"Mm-hmm." Vera, the owner of the Curl Up and Dye, nodded with pinched lips. She was a class regular and a huge gossip.

She heard so much stuff at the beauty salon, sometimes she'd get things mixed up, but not this.

"From what I understand, Zeke was arrested for the protest. Something about it getting out of hand and Zeke threatening Max or something." She shrugged. "Who knows. I guess all of us small business owners are going to have to figure out a way to compete. Did you see the quilts hanging up in there?"

I wasn't sure if Vera used the extra set of knitting needles stuck in her hair as a fashion statement or a hair tool, but I did know her hair was different every single week. This week it was bright red.

While they gossiped about the booths inside of the King Building, I took my time to walk behind the rocking chairs so I could peek over the back to make sure the new students had gotten their blankets started. It was the hardest part, but the yarn we were using for the blanket was a forgiving yarn, so it didn't show too many mess ups. With the cost of the class, they got the blanket pattern, a small measuring spool, a pair of scissors, four yarns of their color choosing, along with US size nine knitting circular needles plus a Stitchin' Post logo canvas bag so they could simply keep all of their class items and project in one place, making it easy for them to transport from home to class and vice versa.

"I love the feel of this yarn." One of the students glanced back at me.

"The one hundred percent merino wool single-ply yarn. It'll make your blanket squishy and soft. You're going to love to cuddle up with it." I looked at her cast-on stitch a little closer, peeling back her initial stitch to make sure she got it started correctly. "Perfect."

There was still more room for progress. It took time and practice to perfect the initial cast-on, something all of them would naturally do as they took on bigger and harder projects.

"Why are we using this type of needle?" Vera stopped gossiping long enough to ask when I walked behind her.

"Your finished blanket is going to be fifty inches wide, and there's no way all those stitches will fit on the standard straight needle. But we will be treating them like they are straight needles." I smiled and moved on after Vera appeared to be satisfied with my answer.

The bell over the front door of the shop dinged.

"Are you expecting someone else?" Sharon's forehead wrinkled as she counted the rocking chairs and saw each one was filled, knowing I would've put out the right amount.

"I thought I locked the door." I shrugged and looked around the

Linden Falls Knitters and new knitters to make sure no one needed anything before I went into the shop to see who was in there.

"I've got this." Sharon put down her knitting project and got up so she could walk around.

Literally. The perfect best friend.

The lowlights in the shop were on, and darkness had fallen in and around Linden Falls due to the autumn time of the year along with daylight saving time. The lack of natural light showed a figure standing at the front.

I flipped the light switch and I saw Pam Olson, one of the local HGTV-type show hosts, standing next to the door.

"I saw a light on in the back and tried the door. It was open." Pam glanced around.

"How can I help you?" I wondered since I'd never seen the woman other than on television when she and Steve Turner cohosted the local renovation show, *Wishes of Home.*

"I was walking past a few minutes ago." She gestured to the sidewalk. "I saw how cute the shop was and noticed the chalkboard sign in the window." She turned back and smiled.

"I'm interested in your knitting lessons for beginners. I saw the throw in the window, and I'd like to make that for my boyfriend for Christmas."

"What a lovely gift." I knew that one particular pattern was going to draw in a lot of new customers.

"Is it really a project for a beginner, and do you think I can finish it by Christmas?" she asked.

"Yes. And yes!" I beamed at Pam. "A throw is a big project, but the yarn is bulky, and the needles required are large."

I gave her a few more particulars about the needles but noticed I was losing her attention because she didn't really care so much about the particulars as much as the finished project.

"Like you were just doing when I came in?" She looked over at the counter at a project I'd been working on. "My grandmother could work a cable stitch without looking. I never knew how she did it."

"Experience and practice," I said matter-of-factly. "Was she a lifelong knitter?"

Pam nodded.

"We have knit-ins here all the time. Joining in would help you stay on track. People drop by with their current knitting project and sit in the classroom in the back." I pointed to the room in the back. "There are several experienced knitters who come, and they help the novices if they drop a stitch or have a problem. I'm always here to help too."

"That sounds nice. Cozy." I could see in her eyes she was very interested.

"It is. We knit and visit and have a good time. If you want the real scoop about what's going on around Linden Falls, come to a knit-in." I picked up one of the flyers I had made up just for the knit-in times and handed it to her.

Pam chuckled. "Really?"

"Ask Calvin over at the *Linden Falls Gazette*. He'll tell you. My knitters knew about the sale of the King Building before Calvin found out about it. And the plan to make it into the artist's display space and event venue." I nodded.

"I heard people talking about it in Duncan's Hardware." She confirmed the rumors.

"Yep. And everyone isn't happy about it. I can tell you that." My brow arched, and I leaned forward a little. "Vendors at the farmers market on Saturday mornings are worried about the competition."

"My mom has sold her handmade table linens and aprons at the market for years. She's not worried about it." Pam shrugged it off.

"You're Irene's daughter." I knew Irene from the knit-ins, but she never told me *the* Pam Olson was her daughter.

"You should come with her to a knit-in," I suggested since it was always easier to come with someone on your first time.

"We have plans on featuring the new King Artisan Market on the show. Max has been great allowing our cameras and crews in there to film while they've done a remarkable job renovating the old King Building." She turned the conversation to their HGTV-style show.

But what did this have to do with me, I wondered as she rambled on about the King Building.

"I have seen an episode or two," I told her as we both continued to walk to the middle of the shop.

"We have gotten such great response, and as you know, we did the segment a while back on Friends for Life. To stop beating around the bush, we've had an unexpected opening for filming tomorrow, and like I said, I was walking by, and it dawned on me that you're the shop who makes the blankets for the shelter." She let go of a long sigh. "I called Steve, and we both agreed that we'd love to come here tomorrow and film a little segment about your shop, take a few pans around the store, and talk about the blankets. We are just really trying to showcase all the local and good things in our community."

"Wow." My brows lifted. "That's fantastic. I'd love to talk about the Stitchin' Post and how we do love to give back to our town."

"Perfect." The pleased look settled on her face as she nodded in agreement. She dug down into her purse and pulled out a business card, handing it to me. "Here is my direct cell phone. If anything changes between now and in the morning, say around ten a.m., call me."

"Ten a.m.," I repeated to make sure we were on the same hour.

"See you then." She left before I could formulate some real questions, which were: what would one wear on television? Did I need to do special makeup, and did I need to have any sort of lighting?

When I went to the door to look out on the street, to see if she was anywhere close for me to ask, she was gone.

There was a smile as big as the King Artisan Market crawling on my face as I looked over at the Wishing Tree, where a few months ago, in the dark of the night, I'd hurried over to the tree, where I had written down and tied a wish: get more exposure for the shop so I could stay in Linden Falls.

Now I knew my wish was going to come true.

I didn't dare tell anyone in the class, nor Sharon, who was at the door, what had happened. Luckily, Sharon didn't ask. She was too busy helping one of the new knitters recast on her needles.

I couldn't stop thinking about it the entire way home. The headlights pointed down the curvy, secluded rural road on my way out of town, where I owned a small cabin near Linden Falls, the actual waterfall the town was named after.

When I first moved here, Sharon wanted me to get an apartment with her, but I knew I wanted my own space, and when I saw the dumpy cabin was for sale and in my price range— cheap—I knew I could make it a home.

Honestly, I loved the surroundings of the cabin more than the dwelling itself. The cabin was very close to the path leading to the falls. During the silence of the night, the echoes of the falls drifted through my open windows and lulled me to sleep. In the spring was when the waterfall was at its loudest and most enjoyable due to the large runoff of the melting winter snow, which brought the most delightful sight of the gorgeous blooming spring flowers.

That time also brought the tourists, who would sit on the large rocks near the waterfall with their picnic lunches to enjoy its beauty. I didn't mind sharing the area.

The car's headlights rolled from the far end of the small cabin when I turned right into the driveway and shined on the front porch when I put it in park.

Vance Stratton was sitting in the rocking chair with Tilly in his lap, moving back and forth.

"I wasn't expecting to see you." I tried to stop the big, teenager-type smile but gave up. "What a pleasant surprise."

Vance and I had been dating for the last five months and getting more serious as the days went by. I'd yet to tell my family about him due to the fact my mom would not just stop at one detail, but she'd go way beyond that and start googling his name, searching him out on social media, and probably try to get a social security check.

It was my little secret in my little town of my little life.

"I got back from my trip a day early and thought I'd make supper for us since I knew you had your knitting class tonight." He got up and walked down the couple of front porch steps, cradling Tilly in his arms

19

so she didn't jump out since we were too close to the road, though she did have the luxury of being an indoor and outdoor cat.

She never left the porch unless I called her to take a walk with me to the falls or I was pulling weeds from my garden bed. Other than that, she was content lying on the porch to catch what little bit of sunlight she could.

Vance kissed me, and I could smell the charcoal on him.

"Are we grilling out?" I opened the back door and took out my knitting bag.

"Steaks." He wiggled his brows. "Nothing too good for my girls." His tone turned a little mushy when he talked to Tilly. "How were the new students?"

"They were great. Sharon helped a lot, and Pam Olson stopped by." I headed into the cabin and hung my keys up on the knitting-needle hook screwed on the wall next to the door. I set my purse on the small table before I thumbed through the stack of mail Vance must've gotten from the mailbox.

"You mean the people from the television show?" Vance's brows knitted. He helped me take off my light jacket and hung it on the hook as well.

"Yeah." I gave him the quick recap of what happened and the show's spotlight on the Stitchin' Post. "She said something about how a spot had become free or available."

"That's wonderful." Vance took me by the shoulders and hugged me. "You deserve this, you know."

"Funny you should say that." We headed into the kitchen, where he'd already put a few vegetables in the oven. The cabin smelled heavenly, and the smell of charcoal wafted through the open windows. "I don't know if I ever told you. When I moved here, I put a wish on the Wishing Tree."

He grinned because he knew when we first met how much of a skeptic I was about the whole thing. I said it was taking advantage of people and giving them hope, but I had to admit when I started to see, firsthand, some of these wishes coming true, there was something inside that felt good and made me want to do good. I'd even taken a look at some of the wishes I could afford and made them come true, anonymously.

"Get this." I watched him pour us a glass of red wine and took the one he handed me. By the looks of the vegetables, I knew we had some time to talk before we ate, so I walked back into the small family room that was big enough for two end tables and a small couch and sat down.

Vance followed me and sat next to me. Tilly wasn't going to be left out. She jumped up on the back of the couch and lay between our shoulders. Vance had already started a fire in the cabin's old fireplace right in front of the couch. It was getting nice and cozy.

"I saw Max this morning at the Wishing Tree, plucking off all sorts of wishes. I wonder if he did mine." I swirled the wineglass in the air to watch the red circle drip down, just for fun. "Think about it. They did the big *Wishes for Home* segment on the King Artisan Market. Now it's wrapped up, he might've taken my wish. But why?" I was trying really hard to come up with the real reason Pam Olson was just walking past my shop and it dawned on her.

"You got the spot, right?" He put his hand on my thigh. I nodded. "Then that's all that matters. The Wishing Tree isn't supposed to be analyzed when your wish comes true. That's the magic of the tree and how it works."

"I guess. But where I'm from, those things just don't happen." I leaned my head on his shoulder and looked at the stone fireplace. The orange-and-red flames danced above the logs.

"It's time for you to enjoy your life. Put down the baggage of your past. It's too heavy. You don't have to do that anymore." The words he spoke seeped into my ears and married my heart.

CHAPTER 4

*M*ewl, mewl. Tilly was better than any alarm clock. And a lot more pleasing to the ears than the loud buzzing.

She lightly touched my nose with her soft paw. Her little toe beans felt cold to the touch.

Mewl. She gave another tap before I opened my eyes and looked at her. That's when she jumped off the bed and darted out of the bedroom door.

Once she saw my eyes open, she knew it was breakfast time.

"I wish you'd sleep just an extra fifteen minutes," I said, sitting up on the edge of the bed, slipping my feet into the slippers. "But a girl has to eat when she's hungry."

I grabbed my robe from the back of the chair next to my bedroom door before I padded down the hallway to meet her in the kitchen, where her bowl sat empty.

Tilly danced around my ankles, curling her tail around my shin as I opened up the kibble food container and dumped a scoop in her bowl.

While she munched away, I lifted the windows in the kitchen and family room to get some good, fresh morning air and cool breeze in while I got ready for work.

A shotgun blast echoed just as I turned on the water to fill the coffee carafe, making me pause. Deer hunting season wasn't for another week. My lips curled together when I heard another shot ring out, a little too close for my comfort, and made me shut the windows. Tilly stopped eating and looked up at me as though she knew it wasn't time too.

"I'll be sure to call Hector today. And you will go to work with me," I told her and decided not to make coffee. The quicker I could get dressed and us out of there, the happier I'd be since someone was obviously hunting too early.

Now, during the hunting season, I did make sure to put out all the things around my property for hunters to know it wasn't hunting land. That's how I knew it wasn't hunting season, and I still had the upcoming weekend to get the orange ties and signs posted.

"You are going to the shop with me today because we are going to be on television." Even though the reality was I didn't want to leave Tilly alone with a poacher in the wooded area for fear something would happen to her.

Plus it would be good for *Wishes for Homes* to see how their other project Friends for Life did bring a companion into my life, which was where the blankets the Stitchin' Post made and donated went to. The full circle moment.

"Full Circle Moment," I said out loud while I put the finishing touches of makeup on. "That sounds like a great title for the segment."

I was pretty pleased with what I'd come up with, and I would definitely suggest it to them.

Tilly knew she was coming with me when she saw me packing up some of her treats and a small baggie full of kibble. She didn't mind the shop and mostly slept in the front display window in the sun.

When we got to the shop, that's exactly where she went, leaving me to do the morning rituals I'd always done. That included going to get my breakfast sandwich from Nicole.

"Are you coming to the Hot Air Balloon festival tonight?" Nicole handed me my brown bag and coffee.

"I'm not sure. Vance got back early." I didn't have to tell them too much about Vance since they all knew he had a traveling job with the web designer company he worked for, and like I said, he was from here so they all knew him very well. "We didn't talk about it."

"You live out by the falls, right?" she asked and glanced over my shoulder when some customers came in. "I'll be right there," she told them when they walked past us.

"I do. Not too far from the path." It hit me that I needed to call Hector about those gunshots.

"If you stand on one of the tallest rocks, you can see the glow of the balloons, and it's gorgeous. There's a lot of photographers who come from all over Vermont to get the shots." She shrugged. "Have a good day."

"Thanks for the food." I took the bag and headed out across the park and looked at the Wishing Tree as I passed by it, wondering if my wish was on there.

I bit the edge of my lip and looked around before I gave in. The lowest limb was where I'd tied my wish. I knew exactly where I'd done it, so I could see if it was ever missing, just to see if this whole thing was real or not.

The lowest limb forked off from the main trunk, and just below that fork there was a blemish on the trunk in the shape of a heart. That's where I had left my wish tied, and when I looked, it was still there.

Or so I thought.

"I knew this wishing thing was wrong." The skeptical words rolled out of my head and out of my mouth. I put the bag of food on the ground and reached up to pluck my wish off. "There. My wish came true without anyone plucking it off." I stuck it in my pocket, grabbing my bag to get back to the shop so I could get it all prettied up for the big segment on *Wishes for Homes*.

Ten o'clock came fast, and when Pam and Steve showed up with all the cameras and equipment, I started to nervous sweat.

"It'll be fine. Just walk around with me and talk to me. Don't look at the camera or try to keep a smile on your face. It's like two old friends are having coffee, and you're telling me about your new shop." Pam tried to put me at ease by making it sound common and easy to do, but there was no part of this that was easy.

"If we need to do a few takes, it's fine," Steve assured me. "We do those a lot. First, I'll ask you about Tilly. That should start to make you feel at ease, and the more you talk about the things you love, you will be more natural than you think."

"And we have a great editing team who will put it all together by slicing it all up to make you look like the superstar you are." Pam, Steve, and I stood there in the middle of the shop.

The crew did what they called micing us up by placing the microphones on our clothing, and before too long, I was telling them the story about Friends for Life, Tilly's story, which led me and the Linden Falls Knitters to make the blankets for the shelter.

They were right. When I started to talk about the things I was passionate about, it all flowed. Easy. And then the camera crew cut off us off in midsentence and called Steve and Pam over, leaving me wondering what was going on. Did I say something wrong? Did I look bad?

Wrong.

"I'm sorry. We have to go." Pam stayed behind to talk to me while the crew and Steve bolted out the door. "We will need to reschedule. There's been a body found at the falls by a tourist, and we have to get the scoop."

"The Linden Falls?" I questioned before Pam got to the door.

"Yes!" she hollered on her way out, almost knocking over Sharon.

"What's going on in here? Did they do a segment on the shop and you didn't tell me?" Her eyes narrowed. "What? What's wrong?"

"Someone was found dead by the falls." The memory of the shots I'd heard this morning rang out in my head. "I forgot to call Hector."

"All of those cameras and crew were here about the body?" Sharon's shoulders drew back, her eyes darkened. "Is there something I don't know about you?" Her eyes shifted to the pair of needles I'd had in my hand while filming the segment about the different types of needles and sizes before they got the call about the body.

"No." When I waved the needles in a gesture to wave off Sharon's comment, she took a step back. "Honestly, Sharon. Do you think I could kill anyone?"

"You're not making a whole lot of sense." She shrugged and reached out, taking the needles and carefully placing them on the counter. "What is going on? Start from the beginning."

"I'm not sure if the beginning was this morning when I heard a couple of shots ring out next to the cabin or if it started later." I could hear the jumbled message coming out of my mouth. I blinked a few times to bring me back to the present. "I think I heard someone get shot this morning while getting ready for work."

Sharon's jaw dropped.

"Do you remember yesterday during class when someone came to the door?" I waited for Sharon to nod. "That was Pam from *Wishes for Homes*. She asked if she could do a segment on the Stitchin' Post this morning. She said she just so happened to walk by and see the sign, thought it was a great idea, and here she was. And for this morning."

"I thought it took weeks to prepare for things like this." Sharon thought the exact same as me.

"Exactly. This morning while Tilly and I were getting ready"—I glanced up to the display window, where Tilly was still curled up on one of the afghan blankets I'd knitted, not a care in the world—"I overheard a shot." I shook my head. "Two shots." I paused to replay the memory before I committed to saying two shots. "Yeah. Two shots, and I know it's a little too early for deer hunting season. Dang it."

I smacked my hands together.

"Did you remember something? Seeing someone?" Sharon asked in a hushed tone when a customer came through the door.

"Let me know if I can help you," I called out. They nodded and smiled. "No. I was going to call Hector and tell him about it because I thought it was odd, but it completely escaped my mind with all the cameras and stuff."

I'd yet to turn on the radio where I liked to play the local station during the day. It was a great mix of music, plus it had hourly weather and news updates.

"Are they going to refilm the segment?" Sharon had moved from the body to the show.

"I don't know. All I know was when they got the call about a body at the waterfall, it clicked that it's what I heard. Had to be." My voice fell away as I made my way behind the counter and flipped on the radio.

"Had to be," Sharon repeated.

"Here's the thing. I don't believe Pam at all about walking past and just so happening to get an epiphany to do a story on the television about the Stitchin' Post." For some reason, my gut told me it was a little too convenient.

"Why not? If anyone in this town deserves a shop showcase, it's you. And all that volunteer work you do for the community. And with a boyfriend." Sharon picked up one of the new skeins of yarn and rubbed it against her face. "So soft. Why don't you make me a blanket with this one?"

"Then I thought about the Wishing Tree."

Sharon jerked to look at it. A wry smile crossed her lips. Slowly, she put the yarn ball back in the basket where it belonged.

"You? Wishing Tree?" she questioned like it was the most off-the-wall thing I'd ever said. "You don't believe in the Wishing Tree. Or do you?"

"To help with my skepticism, I made a wish about the shop and exposure." I put my hand in the pocket of my jeans and pulled out the wish with the string still attached. I slapped it in the palm of her hand. "As you can see, it wasn't taken."

Sharon read the wish. Slowly, she scanned up to my face to meet my eyes.

"I told you it was a scam." My shoulders drew up to my ears before falling back down.

"Whose body did they find?" Sharon asked in a cold tone.

"I'm not sure. Why?" I threw the wish in the trash along with a few scraps of yarn.

Breaking news, breaking news. The DJ broke into the middle of the song on the radio, catching our attention.

"Turn it up!" Sharon hollered out. The sound of the customer jerking around made us remember she was in there. "Turn it up," Sharon whispered as if I'd not heard her the first time.

Both of us stood with our ears leaning into the speakers.

The body found at Linden Falls Waterfall this morning has been identified as Zeke Turner. We don't have all the details, and this is a developing story. Be sure to stay tuned. We will break in with any further news.

"Zeke Turner?" I questioned, swallowing down how we'd just seen him yesterday.

"Did you wish for Zeke Turner to die?" Sharon's voice mysteriously took a downward turn. She flipped the piece of paper my wish was written on to face me so I could see it.

"That's not my wish." I gasped, realizing someone really did wish Zeke's demise, and it was written right there on the paper.

CHAPTER 5

fter talking Sharon off the ledge of thinking I killed Zeke Turner without any sort of motive whatsoever, she'd gone back to work, and I called Hector Norton to let him know I'd heard the gunshots that morning.

He told me he'd send a deputy out to the Stitchin' Post to get my statement, so when I saw Hector himself walk through the door, I was a little taken aback.

"Can we talk in the back?" I asked him before he could ask me any questions about the gunshots.

The shop was filled with tourists and some locals. By the shifty eyes of some familiar faces, I could tell their ears were peeled for any details they could get about Zeke Turner.

Hector followed me back to the classroom, where I offered him a cup of coffee and a seat. Both of us sat in rocking chairs. He took out his notebook and steadied it on his thigh before he started to ask me questions.

"Tell me in your own words what you heard." Hector's jaw was set. His head was slightly tilted as he intently stared at me.

"Well." I gulped. My hands started to sweat. "I was getting ready, and my window in my kitchen was open a little. You know, to let fresh air in." My voice cracked.

Ahem. I cleared my throat.

I continued, "I decided to come to the shop a little early because there was a segment for *Wishes for Home* being filmed here this morning."

"This morning?" He looked up underneath his brows as if he didn't believe me.

"Yes." I nodded.

"Pam and Steve were here?" he asked.

"Yes." I nodded again.

"This morning you heard a gunshot." He wrote it down.

"Two gunshots," I clarified. "Definitely two. That's why I brought Tilly to work. She is an indoor and outdoor cat, and I didn't want anyone mistaking her for something they could kill."

"I see." He looked down at the notepad. "What time was this?"

I rattled off the details and how I'd not heard anything more, so Tilly and I came to work, and that's when I heard it on the radio.

"Do you know who on earth would do such a thing?" I questioned.

"I went to see Zeke's wife this morning to let her know about what had happened. She told me he'd gotten a call last night about his protest in front of the King Artisan Building. When he got off the phone, he told her it was Pam, and she was going to meet him at the falls and do a segment on him and why he protested the market. When he questioned the falls, his wife said he told her Pam mentioned how it was part of the reason why tourists came to Linden Falls as well as the market in the park where the Wishing Tree stands."

"Wishing Tree." I gasped and leaned on my left hip to take the wish out of my pocket. "Speaking of wishes. I've been a little skeptical of the Wishing Tree since I moved here, and I had put a wish on the tree for my shop to get some sort of promotional-type thing to get the word out. Today, when I was walking back from the Crooked Porch with my coffee and breakfast sandwich, I noticed my wish was still dangling on the tree."

I handed him the wish.

"You wished for Zeke Turner to be murdered?" he asked.

"No. Noooo." I shook my head. "It was early, and I knew I tied my wish exactly where that one was hanging. I didn't read it. I figured it was my wish, so I jerked it off the tree. I put it in my pocket and didn't think about it until later in the afternoon."

I left out how Sharon and I had finally read it.

"When I read it, I knew I needed to call you." My brows pinched. "Even though I had already planned to call you about poachers."

"So you're telling me someone wished for Zeke Turner to die?" He wagged the piece of paper.

"Apparently so." My eyes were fixated upon it.

"And you had a wish in that same spot?" He appeared to be confirming that I was fully sure.

"Yes."

"Cheryl." He leaned back in the rocking chair and took a deep breath before letting go of a very long sigh. "I think someone is trying to set you up for the murder of Zeke Turner."

That little bit of news from Hector didn't sit too well with my stomach. In fact, I felt so bad, I'd thought about canceling class. The idea someone would try to make me the scapegoat for Zeke's death was a hard one to take, but when the news announced his death was now a homicide, it became all too real.

"What do you know about Zeke?" I overheard Sharon asking Vera while they were working on their project in the classroom as I tidied up the shop so I could go home.

It was a long day. Even Tilly seemed to know it was time. She'd started to follow me around, meowing, curling her tail around my shin —her way of letting me know she was ready to go home.

"I know, girl." I picked up a ball of unraveled yarn and wound it while I kept an ear peeled to see what Vera had to say.

"You know Zeke wasn't the easiest man to get along with. He wasn't ever happy. Some might think Max could've done it since Zeke had been protesting the artisan market, but Max doesn't hold grudges. Now

Nick Sutton." The name stuck in my head until I made my way over to the counter, where I quickly wrote down Nick Sutton's name. "He and Zeke had major fights over those darn butter beans."

"Butter beans?" Sharon continued to bait Vera, who probably didn't need much encouragement.

"Mm-hmm." I heard her hum as I made my way back to the classroom with my paper in hand. "Of course, Ann told me that yesterday when she came in for a cut and curl at the end of the day. She didn't have an appointment, so I knew she was going to talk about the big rumblings of the body."

"She did mention something about Zeke's landlocked neighbor." Vera sighed and kept her eyes on her needles while she worked the thread.

"Landlocked?" I asked.

"Oh yeah. Apparently, Zeke owns that little bit over five acres out there in the countryside where he and Darlene live." Vera pointed her needle at me. "I'm not sure if you've ever ventured out that way, but you should. He's used up every single piece of land to grow his vegetables for the farmers market, and I mean there's not one piece of grass. He's landlocked and from what I understand wasn't happy about it when the old run-down and empty cottage house is sitting empty."

I guess the confused look on my face caught her attention.

Vera elaborated, "He'd gone to the people who own the land. They live about twenty minutes from here. Next town over in Middleboro." Her eyes shifted from me to Sharon. "I've got some friends over there, and they said Zeke Turner had been going over there to the courthouse to get the records of the deeds. When the next of kin refused to sell him the property, he created all sorts of stink. He demanded to see the tax bill and all sorts of things."

"Do you remember their names?" I asked.

"Charles something or other." Vera looked off as if she were trying to remember. "Charles is the last name. Skye." She clicked her needles together. "Skye Charles. I remember because that's an unusual name, and it reminded me of the bright-blue sky."

"Skye Charles." I wrote that name down when Vera continued to talk so she didn't question why I was writing any sort of information she was giving me down.

When Hector told me how maybe I was being set up or even just my name coming out of Hector's mouth, it made me want to figure out why someone would do this. Not that I'd consider myself any sort of sleuth like you'd read in one of those cozy mystery books, but I was beginning to think that if I wanted answers, I couldn't sit around and wait for Hector Norton to give them to me. Heck, he wasn't the fastest chief of police around, and I didn't want to spend the next few months looking over my shoulder.

Besides, I never liked to be used or accused of something. There was no guarantee anything Vera was saying would amount to nothing but a hill of beans, but at least I could just snoop around and see what these people knew.

"HE EVEN WENT AS FAR as going to the courthouse here to see about getting the cottage condemned, forcing Skye Charles to do something with it, and we all know the ordinance in Linden Falls about keeping everyone's property looking tidy." Vera was right about that.

The town government made sure all the property, whether it was a house, neighborhood, park or even shops, was kept up and looked presentable since our little town was a great destination for tourists.

It was a law that I appreciated.

"Then we have Zeke's stepdaughter. Camille." Vera really got our attention with this little bit of information.

"What about her?" Sharon asked.

"She never liked Zeke since her mother married him. I went to the wedding. I've been friends with Darlene for years." Sharon and I were all ears as Vera recounted the wedding. "Camille showed up at the wedding, throwing around all sort of accusations about Zeke and his philandering ways. But I knew he'd not stepped out on Darlene. Even though Camille has gone as far as putting a tracker on his car. Even a few weeks ago, according to Darlene."

"Wow. That's crazy." Sharon spoke for both of us.

"I wonder if Hector knows this?" I looked at both of them.

Vera pushed back into the rocking chair and used the toe of her shoe to stop rocking.

"Now, we don't need to be meddling in anyone's business." Vera shot me a look. "If Darlene wants him to know, she'll tell him. If you do say something, you don't tell them you heard it from me."

Vera reached down next to her and closed up her fancy yarn holder she could just throw in her bag to keep her yarn from tangling. She pushed her knitting project in the bag and got to her feet.

"I won't be here tomorrow night. We are going to the balloon glow." Vera tossed the bag on her shoulder.

"We are definitely going, right, Cheryl?" Sharon asked.

"Yes. Vance went out of town again today for the rest of the week." I wanted to call him so bad today, but after Hector left the shop, it got busy, and then Sharon and Vera showed up to work on their projects.

Vera waved goodbye and headed out of the classroom.

I was fine with Vance being gone. I knew I'd call him when I got home. The thought of home knotted my stomach worse than any amount of yarn getting tangled.

What if there was someone out there trying to pin something on me by exchanging my wish for the killer's wish?

"What?" Sharon asked. "Your face just went flushed."

I peeked into the shop to make sure I saw Vera leave.

"I swear I saw Max taking wishes off the tree early in the morning." I chewed my jaw in anticipation of what I was about to say about one of the most-liked men in Linden Falls. "The wishes he'd plucked off were exactly where my wish was tied. I can't help but think…" I gulped.

"He replaced your wish and planted it there in hopes to throw Hector off track from looking at him as the suspect since he was the one who called Hector about the protest." Sharon snapped her fingers and put her knitting things in her bag before she got up from the rocking chair.

"But why would Max kill him?" I didn't want to go around accusing people of things as big as murder if there wasn't really a good motive.

"Are you kidding? Money!" Sharon's voice raised. "If you listen to any of those crime podcasts, money is usually the motive. Think about it, Cheryl."

I grabbed the piece of paper, and while Sharon paced back and forth giving me all the details of why Max would have motive, I started to write them down.

"Do you know how much money it cost to purchase the King Building?" she asked and pointed to the paper for me to write down. "The buck doesn't stop there. Then the renovation? The advertising they'd been doing? I heard they've been putting it in papers and online all over the state of Vermont. Not only to get tourists to come but to get vendors to come. I also heard it cost twenty thousand dollars just to rent the place for a wedding."

My jaw dropped.

"Yep. Big money Max is banking on to get his money back from the investment. When you have a local yokel creating all sorts of havoc with protesting and whatnot, then it's time you get rid of them." Sharon brought another question to my mind.

"But why the falls?" I questioned.

"Hector did say you might be getting framed. The falls is by your house, and you go there a lot. Then your wish is gone or replaced?" Sharon had put some good questions and reasoning in my head.

"We also can't forget about Skye Charles." I had a gut feeling Skye Charles was a big player in this whole murder thing. "What are you doing tomorrow?" I asked Sharon.

"I have to work, but I'm starting to feel a little cold coming on." She sniffed a couple good fake ones then coughed. "And a cough."

"Good. I hear there's a great doctor in Middleboro who specializes in such illnesses." I smiled, knowing Sharon was going to stick by my side until we figured out what was happening around here. "Maybe we can stop by the yarn shop there too. I did hear it was nice."

"What time do I need to call in to work?" She grinned, and we set our plans.

CHAPTER 6

$\mathcal{I}$ think I was happier than Tilly when we got home. Sharon had offered for us to come stay the night with her since she could tell I was a little skittish about the whole thing with Zeke.

If I truly didn't want to go home, Tilly and I could've stayed at the Stitchin' Post for the one night, but we were fine. Even if I had to sleep with one eye open, I did feel more comfortable at home.

"You better keep your doors locked," Vance warned on the phone. "I know you think Linden Falls is safe, and you have a habit of forgetting to lock the doors."

"I'll be fine." I bit down into one of the apples I'd gotten at last Saturday's farmers market. "Do you think they'll still have the farmers market in the park?"

"I don't see why not." Vance was always optimistic. One of the qualities I loved so much. "Just because they opened the artisan market doesn't mean they are going to stop letting the locals have the farmers market. Unless the proposal goes through."

"What proposal?" I'd not heard of a proposal. And I probably wouldn't since I wasn't on any sort of town council or committee.

Fur went flying off Tilly's back with each swipe of my hand. Her purrs were deep and loud.

I enjoyed the simple things in life like going to work, coming home, spending time with Sharon and Vance, rubbing on Tilly, then doing the same thing all over again. Nowhere on that list was committees or murder.

"Mayor O'Brien's column in the *Linden Falls Gazette* mentioned it. I didn't read the entire thing. Just scanned it." Vance truly was great about keeping up with the town. "You really should be reading the paper and what changes could be made. You're a business owner. Maybe you should think about joining the chamber of commerce."

"Maybe." I hit the speaker button on the phone and then hit the internet app so I could search for the *Gazette*'s online edition to read the mayor's comments. "Do you really think I am being used as someone's scapegoat?"

"I don't see why you would be. You and Zeke never had any sort of argument or beefs with each other. But I'm a little surprised you decided to do a wish on the tree." Vance knew I'd been pretty dead set against doing any sort of thing.

"It was a whim. I was sitting at the shop, and it was slow. The thought of tucking tail, pulling out the old college degree and dusting it off to find a different job didn't seem so appealing. I looked at those darn wishes blowing in the wind that early morning and decided to give it a shot." I snorted. "I'm not sure if it was a mindset thing, but business did pick up, and now I've got enough in the business account to pay all the bills and have a little left over for the rest of the year."

A few months ago, I was sweating with the real possibility of having to close the shop, but literally things had changed. Then again, so did the season. Knitters and people who wanted to knit picked up in the cozier months of the year. What I called the 'Ber months. September, October, November, and December. The coldest of the months of the year and when you really thought about being cozy. No better way to be cozy than something warm and knitted.

It also taught me a lesson to put money aside for those leaner months. I was growing every day as a business owner. That meant making sure no one pegged me as a killer, even though I had no clear motive.

"You aren't going to do something crazy like try to figure this out? I know Sharon listens to those crime podcasts about normal people like you, where they think they want to solve a murder." Vance was cautious not to say anything negative toward or about Sharon.

"I don't know. We are going to Middlesboro in the morning to check out that yarn shop I'd been talking about—" There was a flash outside of my cabin window that caught my eye.

Mewl. Tilly showed her displeasure at me getting off the couch when I walked over to look out into the darkness.

Vance said something I'd not heard due to the fact I was too busy watching a flashlight dart about.

"Cheryl?" Vance brought me back to the conversation.

"Yeah. Um, let me call you back." I didn't want to tell him why, so I made it up. "Tilly needs something."

I didn't wait to hear him say goodbye. I grabbed Tilly's bag of treats and took one out, handing her one on my way out the door, so I didn't necessarily lie to Vance. She did need a treat for being a good kitty.

I clicked the flashlight of my phone on and headed down the path toward the falls to see who was walking there this late at night.

The emergency 911 button on my phone was at the ready, and Sharon and I already shared GPS location from back in the college days when we were barhopping so we didn't lose each other. I had some comfort in knowing if something happened to me, I could hit 911 and Sharon would give them my location.

The splash of the falls echoed around me, and even if I called out to whoever it was, they might not hear me.

Their light darted all over the big rocks around the falls, and the scene of Zeke's murder had been cleared since it was a highly populated area for tourists. And this could've been a tourist. I wasn't sure. But I did know that I rarely saw anyone there after dark and this close to bedtime.

"Who's there?" Abruptly I stopped when I heard the woman's voice. Her flashlight shone in my direction. "I'll call the law!" she warned.

"I live in the cabin just beyond the trail. I'm just out for a stroll." I gulped, not sure if she was armed and dangerous. "My name is Cheryl Paisley. I have a yarn shop in town."

"The Stitchin' Post?" She knew of me. "My friend Vera goes there."

"Yes. I love Vera." I walked closer and saw it was an older woman. "What are you doing out here?"

"My name is Darlene Turner, and I'm here to look for answers as to why someone would kill my husband." The woman's voice sent chills up my spine.

CHAPTER 7

$\mathcal{T}$he woman was clearly upset, and though I couldn't take away her pain, I could offer her a nice cup of tea or coffee back at the cabin.

"We love cats." Darlene accepted my offer with a bit of coaxing only after I'd suggested we grab the big flashlight I had and I'd go back out to help her.

"I've seen your store. In fact, my friend Vera has tried to get me to take knitting lessons, but I just don't have the patience for it." Darlene tried to make small talk, which was something I was never good at, but I'd always been good with listening.

It was a quality that came along with the patience she was referring to. So many times I'd be taking a knitting class and watch all the participants start to relax, get a little more comfortable and open up about problems or issues or even discuss normal everyday life. It was through knitting I was able to find that deep sense of calm and patience.

"You can always come for friendship." I leaned over the kitchen table, where we'd sat down to sip on the tea and whispered, "You don't even have to know what a needle is. We welcome everyone."

"That sounds nice. I don't have a good group of friends. I've always been with Zeke. We love to garden and work out in the yard." She looked down into her cup. She picked up the string of the tea bag and steeped it a couple of times. "Did you make that?" She threw a chin to the knitted blanket on the back of the sofa.

"I did. It's actually simple to do, and we are making those in class now. It's a beginner's pattern." I could've rambled on about the type of yarn, the needles, and the pattern, but she didn't really appear to be listening. "I'm a pretty good listener if you need an ear. And I'm a stranger, so nothing will leave this house."

She looked up. A faint smile crossed her lips, and she blinked.

"I don't know what I'm going to do without Zeke." Her voice choked. "Did you know him?"

"Yes." I shook my head. "He was very kind to me at the farmers market on Saturdays. When I was the new girl in town, he gave me the best cucumbers I'd ever eaten. He said to slice them up and put them in a jug of water."

"Did he also tell you to add a little salt?" Darlene's shoulders fell just enough for me to tell she was relaxing a little bit.

"He did, but I never did add it. The water is so refreshing that I didn't want to interrupt the taste I was enjoying. Maybe I'll try it next time I get some cucumbers from you," I said.

"I don't know if there'll be cucumbers anymore. It was his favorite, besides the little pumpkins, and I can't imagine him not being there with me over those vines." A large tear fell down her face.

I got up and took the box of tissues from the side table of the couch to bring to her.

"Thank you." She sniffed, plucked one from the box. "Plus I'm not sure what Camille wants to do. I called her and was going to offer us to continue his work, but she sent me to voicemail."

Though I wanted to comfort her, I couldn't help but itch that curious side to see what she had to say about who she might've thought did this, and starting with Camille seemed a good place. Vera had told me and Sharon that Darlene's daughter, Camille, accused Zeke of cheating and even putting the tracker on the car, which made for an unhealthy relationship to say the least.

"Camille is your daughter, right?"

"Mm-hmm." She took a tiny sip that I was sure was to appease me as she didn't seem to have an appetite.

Understandable.

"Camille's father passed away years ago when she was a baby. She didn't even know him. I made sure I had photos of him and told her stories of him as she grew up. When Zeke and I dated, she was so close to him. Then we moved here, and she was a teenager." Without saying it, she was implying Camille's teenage years weren't her best. "She changed. Her personality turned on a dime. Zeke and I blinked one day, and we didn't even recognize her."

Here was where I was able to use the gift of patience and listening. The silent pause between us might've been somewhat uncomfortable, but I knew she'd start talking just so she didn't feel any more than she had to. I simply sipped on my tea.

"I decided not to marry Zeke until she was eighteen. That way if she didn't approve, she was old enough to go out on her own. She did." She snorted and shook her head. "But she came right back. She started to show signs of her old self. You know, just being kind and offering some nice words about the garden. She even got her hands dirty a time or two."

"That's so good. I'm glad they had a nice relationship." I knew it wasn't nice, and then she did what I'd hoped she'd do.

Tell me about the relationship.

"They didn't. That's the problem and probably why she sent me to voicemail. She hasn't even come to the house to say she was sorry about Zeke." Her forefinger grazed the rim of the cup over and over. "I don't know what she heard or who she heard it from, but she got on this tangent about six months ago, saying Zeke had been cheating on me."

I stood up and got the hot kettle off the stove along with the various selections of teas and put them on the table.

She thumbed through the teas and continued, "He never once cheated on me. He might be a gambler when it came to meeting his buddies from the Moose Lodge. But it was nothing but nickels and dimes." She opened the Amber Autumn tea.

I picked up the kettle and tipped it over her cup. The steam of the hot water curled up and around her hand as she put the bag in the water.

The water immediately started to turn orange and filtered into a burnt red in color. Apricot, malt, leather, and caramel smells married into the air around us. Darlene bent down and inhaled deeply before she let out a long sigh. She wrapped both hands around the cup and slowly picked it up.

Leaving the cup under her lip, she looked up and said, "I'm not sure why she'd think such a thing." She took a sip.

"I wanted to let you know I found a wish on the tree that someone had made for Zeke." I wanted to know who she could've thought did this to him.

"Kill him?" She cried out, and with a shaky hand set the cup back on the table. "Hector asked me if I knew of anyone who would want to do this to Zeke, and now that you said there was a wish, I can't help but think it was Nick Sutton." This wasn't the first time I'd heard Nick as a suspect, so I was all ears. "He lives next door, and we are landlocked. He is too. He's been after Zeke to sell the small five acres we have, which isn't something we wanted to do. When Max held the town meeting about the King Building, Nick was all for it even though we all told him the prices were going to go up. He and Zeke had actually put their differences aside in order to protest the artisan market because neither we nor Nick could afford to set up in there with the prices Max is charging."

"Funny thing," I said. My head tilted, and my brows furrowed. I took my knitting bag off the back of my chair and took out my needles. Mindlessly, I started to work on my project so she'd feel a little more comfortable and hopefully come to the Stitchin' Post for conversation and friends. "I saw Nick at the new market, and he was selling his butter beans. The prices were too steep for me."

"You didn't buy any?" she asked.

"No. He seemed a little disappointed, but Sharon told him in no uncertain terms that we would have to settle for the frozen kind at the grocery." I couldn't remember exactly what Sharon told him, but Darlene got the gist.

"Zeke told me after I went to pick him up down at the jail, after Hector hauled him in for putting together the protest." She rolled her eyes and continued, "That's when he told me Nick was in there. Do you think it was by coincidence Nick came down to the station right after me? He said he was coming down to get Zeke out of jail. Do you think he was really coming down there to get him out of jail?"

"Over butter beans?" I asked and didn't look at her on purpose so it didn't seem like I was meddling.

"No. Over the land. Zeke told me Nick offered him money again for our five acres because he knew we couldn't grow his garden any more than we already do, which means our income will stay the same, but if he bought our five acres, he could expand and grow. We couldn't offer him any money. We live paycheck to paycheck." Darlene frowned. "He called Zeke right before Zeke left the night he never came home." Her voice cracked. She plucked another tissue from the box and held it under her nose. She looked away.

My heart broke for her. I put my needles down into my lap and reached across the table, placing my hand on hers.

"Did you tell Hector this?" I wasn't pointing fingers, but it sure did seem like Nick Sutton had a reason he wouldn't leave Zeke alone. Was it enough for murder? I wasn't sure. Did they have an argument that got heated and one thing led to another? There were so many questions I had that really needed to be answered.

"I'm not sure, now that I think about it. I've been in shock since this happened to Zeke, and it's like my mind continues to remember things." Her eyes dipped, and she looked up at me. "Some of the stuff I'm telling you are things I'm just remembering." She gave a hint of a smile. "Somehow, you make me feel at ease." She snorted. "It sounds silly, but maybe it's the tea."

"I think you'd really benefit if you come to the knit-ins. You'll find

45

instant friends like me there, and we have plenty of tea." I wanted to give her a place of comfort because I knew over the next few months, and even for the rest of her life, she was going to need good friends and someone to lean on.

"I know you have Camille, but sometimes you just need girlfriends." I offered her another fill-up on her tea. She declined.

"I guess I better get out of your hair." She planted her hands on the table and pushed up to stand.

"Don't you want to go back and look around with my flashlight?" I was kinda looking forward to going out there to see if we could find anything the police didn't. Not that I didn't believe they didn't do their job, but the lingering comment from Hector about the killer using my shop or even me as a scapegoat worried me, and if I could find anything that would lead to the killer, that would be good.

"No. I think I'm just tired now and want to go home." She shook her head. The circles under her eyes darkened. "I parked down toward the beginning of the path to the waterfall where everyone parks."

"I can drive you down there." I got up, but she stopped me.

"You don't need to do that. I'm fine, and I can use the extra time out there by myself. Gets my head straight." Her shoulders slumped. "That's what Zeke used to say when we'd go hiking. He'd say, 'Darlin'.'" She smiled at the memory. "He called me Darlin' instead of Darlene."

"That's a very sweet memory to hold onto." I tried to offer any kind words to help ease the hurt written on her face.

"'Darlin', let's go hiking so we can clear our heads.'" An audible sigh left her as if she were trying to let go of some pain. "I think I'd like to try to clear my head."

"Okay, but here's my phone number if you need anything." I turned around and scribbled my name and number on the scratch pad on the counter. "Anything," I reaffirmed and handed her the piece of paper.

"I will." She started toward the door.

"Can I ask you one more thing?" I couldn't help but wonder if she knew about Skye Charles. "Did you know anything about Skye Charles from Middlesboro? She owns the land on the opposite side of Nick?"

"I've never met her, but I do know she didn't want to sell her land to Zeke at a reasonable price. He came home mad, saying how if Linden Falls cares so much about what everyone's property looks like, then they need to tear down the cabin on her property." She put her hand on the door handle. "Gosh. I never realized just how many people Zeke did have tiffs with until I said all of it out loud. Most of the time, I'd just shrug it off and let him blow off steam. Then he was fine after about an hour."

"Did you tell Hector about her?" I questioned, knowing Sharon and I were going to go to Middlesboro tomorrow to see what we could find out. I really wanted Hector to hear everything from her so he could do his own investigating.

"No, but I will. It seems like he needs to know all of Zeke's issues with others. I guess any one of them could've done this to him." She blinked rapidly. It appeared as if her mind was going a million miles a minute. "It's a shame tomorrow is the balloon glow. Zeke really did enjoy it."

She stepped out on the porch of the cabin and quickly disappeared into the night.

CHAPTER 8

*S*haron had picked me up bright and early to drive to Middlesboro. I'd barely gotten the coffee brewed, and she was standing at the door with her Linden Falls sweatshirt on.

"There are news stations from all over Vermont downtown this morning. All of them wanting to see if Max shows up at the King's Artisan Market." She walked into the cabin and sat down on the couch.

"Really? Because of Zeke's murder?" I asked and unplugged my cell phone from the counter so I could toss it in my knitting bag, which I carried more than my actual purse.

"Apparently, it's going around town how everyone suspects Max, and he's going to give his own press conference." Her brows lifted. "Maybe we should stay around here today and watch all the action."

"I don't think you'll think that after I tell you about my conversation with Darlene Turner last night." I caused Sharon's eyes to grow bigger. "Come on. I'll tell you in the car."

Sharon and I sipped on the coffee I'd made us in the thermoses on the drive to Middlesboro while I told her all about my visit with Darlene.

The conversation spurred Sharon to rattle off all the suspects we'd thought would be good for Hector to investigate, and depending on what we found out today, we'd go to him and tell him what we thought.

"What did Hector say when it came to setting you up?" Sharon glanced at the GPS on her phone when it chimed. She needed to take the next exit off the interstate.

"He said it was possible someone took my wish off the tree and replaced it with theirs. I can't help but wonder if I'd really seen Max take the wishes off that morning or if it was someone else." I glanced out the window at the Welcome to Middlesboro sign right off the exit. "I didn't see anyone replace the wish, and that wish was exactly where I'd tied mine."

"Did you see anyone around that same area of the tree after you saw Max that morning?" Sharon asked something I'd gone over a million times in my head.

"The shop got so busy that day, I didn't get time to go to the bathroom, much less watch the Wishing Tree and all the tourists and locals who go there daily to read the wishes or take photos." My jaw dropped. "Sharon."

"What?" She jerked around.

"Photos. Do you know how many people take photos in the park on any given day?"

"You scared me. I thought I drove out in front of someone," she said and looked in the rearview. "You're right. Someone might have a photo. How do you suspect we get to those people?"

"I don't know. Maybe Hector can ask the public to submit any photos they took the day of Zeke's murder for them to look at." I gnawed on my cheek, thinking it was a good idea, but Sharon was right. How on earth was Hector going to even get people to turn them in, and what were the odds of someone actually having a person in the background of their photos, tying a wish on the tree before I'd gotten there?

"Where is the courthouse?" I took my phone out of my knitting bag so I could look up Skye Charles's address.

"I went to Linden Falls county clerk's office yesterday and pulled the deed of the land she owns next to Zeke. Then I googled her." Sharon tapped the GPS. "She's a local realtor, and we are going to her office. They open at eight a.m."

"You honestly should be a private investigator or something in that field," I jokingly suggested. "Not that you aren't a good architect."

"I love this stuff. Just like I love those crime podcasts." Her voice was gleeful with the possibility of what we might find out. "I can't have someone going around trying to harm my best friend."

"I don't think anyone is harming me." I didn't let Hector's thought really bug me too much. "I think someone simply tied the wish in the same spot, and we need to find out who."

A few minutes later, Sharon parked her car in the real estate office parking lot. Neither of us had any clue what we were going to say, so we figured we'd wing it.

"Hi," I greeted the woman at the front desk. There was a long hallway behind her, and from what I could see, there were a couple of doors on each side. One of them had the unisex bathroom sign. "We are looking for Skye Charles."

"I'm sorry. She's out with some buyers all day, looking for a house." She handed me a piece of paper and a pen. "If you write down your name and number, I'm more than happy to give her the message."

"You don't have a phone number for her?" Sharon butted in, taking the piece of paper from me and giving it back to the woman.

"We don't give out Skye's phone number. But if you're interested in a property and would like immediate assistance, I can get you a cobroker to help you." In no uncertain terms, she let us know Skye was the big dog around here, and no one was touching her unless we went through the proper channels.

"We will come back." I smiled and gestured for Sharon to walk out of the office, even though she gave me a little push back.

"I think we need to push her a little more and tell her Skye is a suspect." Sharon stood outside on the sidewalk in front of the office.

"Act like cops or something?" I joked, but Sharon loved the idea.

"Why not?" She threw her hands up.

"Your sweatshirt looks like a tourist sweatshirt for one, and for two, we don't have any sort of ID to go along with it, and three, it's illegal to impersonate a police officer." You'd think my third point alone would make her not want to do it, but it didn't change her mind.

"Yeah. I guess we'd need some fake IDs." She appeared to be thinking on the idea before I stopped her.

"Come on. We can at least go to the yarn shop." I tugged on the sleeve of her sweatshirt and walked back toward the parking lot.

"It's just a block this way." She pointed down the street. "It's a nice fall afternoon. Not too chilly for a walk."

"Maybe the fresh air will help us come up with another idea to get in touch with Skye." I did like the idea of stretching our legs a bit.

"What if we went to see Neva?" Sharon's mind must've really used up some of the fresh air. "I mean, she does keep the books of all the wishes and people register them with her."

"Sharon," I gasped. "Why didn't I think of that?"

"Why didn't Hector think of it?" She smiled so bright. "See, exactly why I might be good at this private investigation thing."

"Don't quit your day job," I said before I swung the door of the yarn shop open.

It was settled.

On our drive back to Linden Falls and with two bags of new yarn we didn't need, Sharon and I had decided to go downtown to the park for the balloon glow event and pop in to see Neva, the owner of the local inn and the official keeper of the wishes.

When Sharon had gotten sidetracked at the very first balloon, I knew I had to go see Neva on my own because there were at least ten balloons to see and very little time to do it in.

Tethered hot air balloons were lit up all over the park. Linden Falls didn't stop there. There was carnival food and games. Everyone was having a wonderful time taking in the magnificent balloons as they lit up the dark fall night, not even giving the murder of Zeke Turner a thought.

Unfortunately, it was still in the front of my mind, and making my way around the crowd to the inn was my number one priority.

I'd not thought about Neva enjoying the late night at the balloon glow, so when I went into the inn, she wasn't there. The young woman working at the desk, however, said she was more than happy for me to take a look at the wish books.

I knew exactly the one I'd written my wish in, so I knew the wish tied on the tree in my vacant spot had to be after me, unless they'd held onto their wish before they tied it on.

Carefully I flipped through the book I'd written my wish in and scanned down the page, looking for my handwriting. Page after page I flipped through and noticed all the wishes everyone had.

Most of them were for other people or to do good. As I continued to flip, I wondered what kind of person would actually put a wish on the tree about someone's demise.

I gnawed on that thought until I found my wish. I ran my finger over it and smiled, thinking about how it almost came true with the segment of *Wishes for Home*.

"There you are." Sharon sounded out of breath when she walked into the inn to find me with the wish book. "I looked up, and you were gone."

"You were talking, and I didn't want to hurry you, so I decided to come get a look for myself." I pointed to the page where I'd written my wish. "Here's my wish." She looked over my shoulder. "I don't think the person who added the wish about Zeke's demise actually put it in the wish book."

Sharon took the book from me and flipped a few pages past mine.

"In fact, none of the wishes in that book are negative."

"What are you trying to say?" she asked.

"I wonder if someone wanted me to find the wish. I mean, I've been very vocal about how I was skeptical about the Wishing Tree, and all of a sudden, mine was about to come true. When I went to pluck the wish off the tree, my actual wish was replaced." It sounded crazy. I knew that, but somehow someone wanted me to know what they'd done or somehow tie this to me.

"Didn't you say Pam told you they were going to do a segment on the new artisan market but had to cancel with Max because of the protest or something?" Sharon asked. I nodded. She held out the wish book. "Look at the name a few below your name."

"Max." I gasped and looked up. "Sharon, what if Max, who I swear I saw that morning at the tree, saw my wish, plucked it off and replaced it with the wish about Zeke? Then he cancelled the segment, making my wish come true, knowing I'd go out there to see if my wish had been granted. I'd find the replaced wish."

"I think so, too, but the real question is: Why would he do that and make himself a suspect?" Sharon questioned.

"Only one way to find out." I took the book from her and snapped it shut.

"Go see Max?" she asked with hesitation. I nodded. "I was worried you were going to suggest that. But I have to tell you, I talked to Nick Sutton. He was standing over at the hot air balloon that looks like stained glass. It's truly spectacular up close." She put both hands in the air for effect. "You ought to go see it. Really."

"I'm sorry. I've been a little busy looking up wishes." I decided to drop it. "What did Nick say?" I asked on our way back across the park and through the large balloons on our search for Max.

"He said Max gave him a discount for the booth in the artisan market. He also gave Zeke the same discount. Nick said it was a no-brainer to try for the month to see if he could make up enough money to keep the booth in the market. He also mentioned the farmers market was still going to be open on Saturdays and looked at the artisan market as an extra for the week." Sharon waved to people she recognized as we passed them.

She continued, "He said Max presented the idea by explaining to him how tourists were here all week long, and most times they left on Saturday, which means they didn't frequent the farmers market. With the King Building open all week long, they would be able to capitalize on the tourists daily."

"I wonder how much Nick made at the opening?" I asked.

"I asked him." Sharon nodded her head. "He said he is extremely happy with the outcome of extra income, which he was shocked about."

"Max makes a good selling point. I didn't even think about the clientele the King Building would've brought during the week." I shrugged and looked up at all the glowing hot air balloons as they lit up the sky above the park. The Wishing Tree's outline looked so pretty among them.

"I also asked him where he was the morning they found Zeke. He said they were setting up the booth, and there were many people there to give him his alibi." Sharon's lips duck-billed. "I guess he's not the killer."

"Sounds like he's not, but it doesn't mean Max didn't write the wish." I recalled the early morning hour when I saw him pulling wishes off the tree. "I swear it was Max that morning."

"It doesn't make sense it's him, if he's still making money." Sharon huffed. "But we can go ask because I saw him and Janie over at the caramel apple stand."

Sharon and I beelined it over to the stand where, sure enough, we found Max and Janie talking to a few other townsfolk.

"Good evening." I nodded to everyone in the group to give them a proper greeting.

"It's a gorgeous night." There was glee in Janie's voice. "I hear you have a wonderful Christmas blanket for beginners right now."

"I do. You should join us." The more the merrier.

"Vera, at the Curl Up and Dye, told me it's a great group of women and friendship." Janie grinned.

"I told Janie she needed to come take some knitting lessons." Max joined in our conversation. "She would make an excellent addition."

"You don't even have to knit to be a member," I told her and laughed. I moved my attention to Max. "Can I talk to you privately for a minute?"

"Sure you can. I hope you're going to take me up on my offer about a booth in the King Artisan Market." He wasn't about to give up on the idea.

"No, but I do want to ask you about the market." I nibbled on my bottom lip, not sure how to start the conversation without blurting it out how I saw him with my own eyes at the Wishing Tree.

I took a lesson from Sharon and just ripped off the adhesive bandage.

"It's about Zeke Turner." I noticed his body stiffen. "You know he passed away."

"You mean was murdered?" Max's brows lifted. He crossed his arms in front of him and stared down at me. "I told Hector this town was going to crumble around him and us if he didn't find the person responsible. Even if Zeke and I didn't see eye to eye on business, we were still friends."

"About the non-eye-to-eye stuff..." Here went nothing. "I understand Zeke was not happy about the market, and I did witness the argument the other day during his protest."

"Are you beating around the bush, trying to accuse me of killing Zeke Turner over a little protest?" He snorted like it was the most unthinkable thing in the world.

"Not necessarily so much murder, but maybe you saw something that morning when you were plucking wishes off the Wishing Tree." I noticed his sudden change in body language as his shoulders slumped. "My wish was taken but replaced by another one that wasn't registered with Neva in the wish book."

The details of how I knew about the wish not being registered truly didn't matter at this moment.

"I saw you at the tree, pulling off the wishes."

"I was hoping nobody saw me." He pulled his lips together and used a head gesture to follow him a couple more steps away from the group. A little more privacy. "I did, and let's just say I didn't want anyone to see me. I talked to Janie, and we wanted to give back to Linden Falls as much as it's given back to us. She suggested we pull some wishes off the tree and grant them anonymously."

My heart sank. Of course he wasn't the killer. How on earth could I accuse him of such things?

"I was going to the King Building to open up early so the vendors inside could get their booths ready. It was a perfect time to grab some wishes since no one would see me that early. It's all about keeping it a secret for me and Janie." He reached around into his back pocket and pulled out his wallet. He opened it and took out five wishes.

He handed them to me. I found mine in the group and noticed the check mark.

"What's the check mark?" I asked.

"That means we did it or started the process of having it completed. I already had a segment booked with Pam for the *Wishes for Home*. In fact, I've got a couple booked, but Janie and I thought it would be great to have one of those segments go to your wish. I called up Pam, and she took a stroll to your shop that night." His eyes softened.

"I don't know what to say." I knew she didn't just happen to walk by and see the chalkboard sign in the window.

"You don't need to say anything. I just hate it that you know it was us." He put a hand on my arm. "We really have heard great things about the Stitchin' Post, and we want you to do really well."

"Thank you." I put my hands to my heart. "This community has been a lifesaver for me. The people here have been so good and welcomed me with open arms." I got a little teary-eyed.

"I'd appreciate it if you didn't tell Janie you know it was us because it would break her heart." He smiled at me again and looked over at her lovingly. "She is going to come down there. She told me she wanted to learn to knit."

"She's more than welcome. Anytime." I made sure he knew how grateful I was for his generosity.

"I talked to Pam, and she told me the segment got put on hold due to what happened with Zeke." He rocked back on his heels. "She assured me she was going to reschedule."

"Thank you again." I couldn't stop the smile from the generosity and love I was feeling for the community.

"And about Zeke. He and I had our differences, but I even told him that I would close down the King Artisan Market on Saturdays for the farmers market. It probably wouldn't've been good for business, and I might've had to give some booth owners some money back for that time, but I was willing to try to make everyone happy." He looked over when Janie called his name.

"You better go," I told him as Janie waved him over.

"One more thing." He pointed at me. "You should come to the chamber of commerce meetings. It's for the small business owners, and you have a voice. Heck." He shuffled the toe of his shoe across the top of the grass. "You just might be the president one day."

Max excused himself, and I followed him.

"Cheryl." Janie got my attention. "Sharon just talked me into coming to the Linden Falls Knitters."

"Great!" I was happy to hear this. "You're going to love it."

The small group dispersed.

"Did you ask him?" Sharon questioned as we walked away.

"I did." I looked around my feet as the glow of the balloons had made it look as though we were walking on a mosaic floor instead of grass. "Max isn't the killer."

"I didn't think so." She tugged her phone out of her pocket and looked at it. "Say, do you mind if I go hang out with Truman? He is here and asked me if I wanted to go up in one of the balloons."

"No. Go!" I was so excited for her. She'd been wanting to go out with him for so long.

Sharon hurried off just as my phone chimed a text. It was Vance. He couldn't make it back into town from his business trip but would stop by and see me tomorrow on his way into town.

Instead of hanging around the park, I headed home, where Tilly was already curled up on the couch. I joined her and thought about the suspects I thought had the most motive to have killed Zeke Turner.

Nick Sutton. No.

Max. No.

Skye Charles. Possibly.

I took another look at my phone log to make sure I'd not missed a call from her.

Nope.

She was still on my list.

CHAPTER 9

*I*t was hard not to stare over at the Wishing Tree while I tried to unbox the yarn I didn't get to. I knew the shop would have a lot of walk-in customers today since the town was filled with tourists who'd attended the balloon glow last night.

Long gone were the balloons from the park, but the tree still stood majestic with wishes blowing in the early morning breeze.

The weather had turned downright cold, as though Mother Nature had turned the air conditioner as high as it could go. The kind of frigid air before a snowstorm cold. The kind of cold that gave you the desire to stay inside by a cozy fire with a cup of hot something—for me, it was coffee or tea—while you worked the balls of yarn into a nice snuggly blanket. This was the time of year those feelings pretty much lay on everyone's heart who'd even had a little notion they'd love to knit. And the time of year that brought those customers in, which was why I had to get the new fall colors out before we opened.

I forced myself not to look out at the tree and get lost in thoughts of Skye and the lengths she had to go through in order to put a wish on the tree about Zeke—if she were the killer.

Time quickly passed, and before too long, as I was cutting up the cardboard boxes so they'd fit into the dumpster better, the bell over the door *dinged*.

"I'll be right with you," I called from behind the counter, where I'd been sitting on the floor with the stacks of cardboard.

"Take your time," Vance called.

I popped to my feet.

"What are you doing here?" It was so nice to see him this early, and those cups of coffee he was carrying made my mouth water.

"I just got back into town and thought I'd drop by to have coffee with you since I couldn't make it back last night." His grin sent my heart soaring. He held one of the coffees over the counter. "This one has a little bit of almond milk."

"Thank you." I took it from him, our fingertips met, and both of us smiled. "We need to make up for last night. What about you come over tonight for dinner? I'll make us something."

"Are you sure? After a long day here you might want to go out." His idea was appealing, but I wanted some alone time with him.

"Yes. Of course. It might be around eight or so, but I'll be cooking you something." I had to stop by the store and even thought I might stop by to see Darlene after work to check on her and possibly buy some produce. The least I could do was to help ease some of her burden by buying some vegetables.

Not a big part, but it was what I could do.

My phone rang. I flipped it over from the countertop to see who it was, and although I didn't recognize the number, I knew the town.

"Excuse me for one second." I held up my finger and took the Middlesboro call in the classroom. "Hello?"

"Is this Cheryl?" the woman asked.

"It is," I confirmed.

"I'm Skye Charles, and I understand you stopped by the real estate office about some property yesterday." She called me back. I couldn't believe it. "I have some time in about an hour if you want to stop by the office and chat."

"An hour?" I bit my lip and wondered how I would make it happen. "You can see me in an hour?"

"Pst," I heard Vance call out. "I can watch your shop for you if you need to go to an appointment."

"No," I mouthed, waving my hand from the door of the classroom.

"Really. I'm fine. See." Vance made me smile when he took the stack of yarns from the countertop where I'd taken it out of the last box and he started to stick them in the color-coordinated baskets. "I'll be fine."

"Yeah. Okay," I told Skye. "I'll see you in about an hour."

We clicked off the phone, and on my way to the counter, I tried to come up with some sort of reason why I needed to leave now in order to make the drive and be there in time.

"Are you sure?" I asked Vance.

"Yes. I'm sure." He leaned down and kissed my cheek. "Are you okay?"

"It's not a doctor's appointment. I have to go to Middlesboro." I shrugged and walked back behind the counter to grab my knitting bag, where I'd thrown my wallet and keys. "For some yarn."

"Yarn?" he scoffed.

"Mm-hmm. I have some yarn to pick up from when Sharon and I went there. The shop didn't have it, but it's there now." Oh gosh. What kind of person was I? I was lying to him, and it probably wasn't even necessary. "Let me take that back."

Vance curled his arms across his chest and waited.

"I am going to Middlesboro to meet with Skye Charles, the realtor who apparently owns the property next to Zeke and Darlene. I'd heard she and Zeke had differences, and now that there doesn't seem to be any clear suspect in town, I think she might be one." I stopped talking. At this point I wasn't making any sense.

"Why do you think you need to solve Zeke Turner's murder?" He asked a very good question.

"Because someone put a wish on the tree where mine was hanging. It wished for Zeke to die. At first, I thought someone had meant to tie it there for me, to see if I checked to see if my wish was gone, but my mind ran wild. Sharon encouraged me to more than she needed to in order to get my curiosity up, and, well, I just need to know what Skye knows." There. I said it out loud about how I'd gotten myself in too deep, and my curious side now had to be scratched like a bad case of poison ivy.

"M'kay." He shrugged and walked behind the counter.

"That's it?" I asked and watched him hoist the stack of cardboard up.

"Sure. You're an adult. I'm guessing you aren't going to put yourself in danger." He headed toward the back door of the shop. "I'll see you when you get back."

"Yeah." I smiled. Glad to know he wasn't one of those guys who didn't want me to stick my nose where it didn't belong. "I might stop by Zeke's house and pick up some vegetables from Darlene for our supper," I called back to him before he walked out the back door where he was headed to the garbage dumpster.

The drive didn't seem as long as it had when I rode with Sharon. Maybe it was the fact I'd kept my mind busy going through the conversation I'd had with Darlene. Trying to pick apart everything she'd said in case there was a clue there somewhere.

There was a parking spot in front of the real estate office. The same young woman sat at the front desk, guarding the hallway, from when Sharon and I had come to see Skye.

"Hello." The young woman was a little more upbeat today. "Skye said that you might be back." She picked up the receiver of the phone and punched in a few numbers. "Hold on just a second."

She twisted her head away from me and whispered into the phone.

"She'll be here in a minute." She gave a quick smile before she went back to what she was doing when I came inside.

I stood there watching down the hall and put on a friendly face when the woman I could only assume was Skye was walking toward me.

"Cheryl?" Immediately she stuck her hand out. "I'm Skye. Why don't you follow me back to my office."

She didn't leave any room between her sentences for me to even confirm who I was much less say why I was there.

"Do you know what size house you're looking for? We can start with that, then narrow it down." She held the door and gestured for me to walk into her office ahead of her.

I took the first seat I came to and sat down with my knitting bag nestled in my lap.

Skye walked around her desk and sat down, pulling out a few folders from the desk top drawer.

"Do you know how many bedrooms?" She tapped the folders. "I have some great properties getting ready to come on the market. You can have first dibs."

"As enticing as it sounds, I'm not here to buy a home." My words caused her to twist her head and ease back into her chair.

"I'm from Linden Falls." I took a breath.

"I love Linden Falls. I used to live there. In fact"—her eyes narrowed —"I'm trying to get in touch with a client. Zeke Turner."

I gulped.

"I can see you know him. Have you seen him lately?" She scooted to the edge of her desk chair. "He wanted to finalize a contract on some property here in Middlesboro. I'm not so sure his stepdaughter even gave him my messages."

"Here? Middlesboro?" I didn't expect to hear Middlesboro. "You mean the cabin and property next to his house in Linden Falls?" I didn't even touch the stepdaughter comment.

"That dump? No way." She shook her head and twisted around to the credenza. She pulled out a drawer and ran her finger along the tabs. "I can't sell it. I can't even give it away. I can do that because it's my property."

"You own it?" My ears perked.

"Zeke didn't tell you?"

"I'm sorry to tell you this, but Zeke Turner was murdered." The words were so bitter as they left my mouth.

"I'm sorry." She turned her ear slightly to me. "I thought I heard you say 'murdered.'"

"I did," I confirmed. "Darlene is a friend of mine, and I am trying to help make sense of all of this."

Not a lie, I told myself.

"I didn't know you owned the property next to them."

Skye continued to look at me. Her eyes blinked rapidly.

"I thought Zeke wanted to purchase the property." I could tell she was shocked, which told me she didn't kill him, or she was a great actress.

"Yeah. I, um, I'm sorry. I'm stunned." She looked away and sucked in a deep breath. "The land next to him and Darlene is junk. It's in the creek floodplain, and grass barely grows. It's no good for growing a garden. I got a new listing on a ten-acre property here with a garden already started. It's perfect for him to expand. He was trying to get the new owners of the King Artisan Market to open in the spring when he and Darlene could have some sort of crop with the new land to invest in a booth there."

"He was going to buy the land here in Middlesboro?" I asked.

"Yes. They were going to sign the contract. From what I understand, Zeke had to use their savings for their down payment. They'd be able to triple their investment with his vegetables because the soil is perfect." She opened the file and shoved it across the desk. "There're photos of the land in there. Perfect for what they wanted it for."

I opened the file and thumbed through the photos. It was a lovely piece of property, and it would've been a great solution to Zeke's land-locked problem.

"I knew he was having a hard time with the new market opening and feared their livelihood was going to be pulled out from under them. Do you think his death had something to do with all of his vocalization against the project?" she asked.

"The owner of the new market has an alibi." I pointed to the photos. "Do you mind if I take some pictures of these with my phone?"

"You can have the whole file. It's on the market, so anyone can go on the real estate site and print them." The edges of her lips slightly ticked up. "I sure do hate this."

"Yeah, me too." I closed the file and stuck it in my knitting bag.

"You knit?" She changed the subject and pointed to my bag.

"I own the Stitchin' Post in Linden Falls." Just telling her I owned my own shop sent us down another twenty-minute conversation about small businesses and what it took to run one, until I finally got up to leave. "You should come to the knitting club one night," I invited her.

Skye was gracious enough to tell me she'd think about it, but I knew I'd not be seeing her anytime soon.

CHAPTER 10

"Any luck?" Vance asked when he answered my phone call.

"No. She had no idea Zeke had died." My voice fell away. "He was trying to better himself and his life with Darlene by purchasing ten acres in Middlesboro."

"Middlesboro?" Vance questioned it just like I'd done.

"According to Skye, the realtor, she said the land there had a growing garden already so it would be easy for him to continue his garden and have room to triple it. But he still wasn't happy about the market opening due to the fact he couldn't afford it." I gripped the wheel and looked in the rearview mirror at Middlesboro fading behind me. "He was actually trying to delay the opening of the King Artisan Market, not stop it. He needed time to get some crops growing so he could continue to sell. Now that the market is open, he was afraid no one would come to the farmers market on Saturday because they'd get what they needed from someone different during the week."

"Poor guy. So you don't think she killed him?" Vance asked.

"No. I don't." I glanced over at the file sitting on the passenger seat. "It is a nice piece of property. When I stop by to buy some vegetables from Darlene, I think I'll ask her if she's still going to move there."

"Just in case you were wondering, the shop has been doing great. I even upsold someone." He was so proud of himself.

I smiled. I'd never met a guy who didn't knit that sounded as happy as he did that he sold some knitting products.

"I just might have to steal you from your job and hire you," I teased. "I'll see you soon."

I didn't realize soon was sooner than I thought due to the fact when I got to Darlene and Zeke's farm, Darlene was there, but Camille answered the door.

"Can I help you?" the young woman asked. She held her hands over her eyes to shield them from the afternoon sun. Definitely looked as if I'd woken her up.

"Is Darlene here?" I asked. Not sure if this was Camille, I asked, "You're Camille?"

"I am, and no, she's not here." She started to shut the door. I put the toe of my shoe in the doorjamb, stopping it. "Excuse me." She squinted.

"I wanted to get some vegetables, and I talked to your mom yesterday." I didn't say she said I could get some vegetables, I simply said I wanted some. "I mean buy some vegetables."

"She didn't say anything." Camille held the door tight to my shoe, not budging. "She's gone out to plan for what's-his-name's funeral. I'll tell her you stopped by."

"You need my name." I smiled and jammed more of my shoe into the space between the door and the jamb. "Cheryl Paisley."

"The knitter lady. She did mention you." Camille relaxed a little. The door wasn't pressing up against my shoe, but she didn't open it any farther. "I guess you were asking all sorts of questions about Zeke's murder."

"I sure hate it for your family." I had the file of the property in my hand and wagged it at her. "But I love the property they were buying."

She glanced at the folder before sliding her eyes back up to meet mine.

"They?" She scoffed. "You mean Zeke. He was good at spending my mom's money, and I have no respect for a man like that. If you'll excuse me now."

"But your mom wanted to move, and shouldn't you love her enough to accept that what makes her happy is good?" I didn't have the nerve to come out and ask if Camille herself had killed Zeke, but I did know by the way she was acting, if she didn't do it, she'd probably thank the person who did.

"My mom was much happier before he wormed his way into our lives." She jerked her head when she heard barking. "I've got to go. I think our dogs got out."

She slammed the door, not caring that she almost cut off my toes.

I stood there with the door closed in my face, listening to the dogs barking. Camille's voice echoed from the back of the house, yelling for the dogs. The more she yelled, the more it sounded as if they were running farther and farther away.

I walked to the edge of the house and looked around the corner to see what all the commotion was about after I'd heard more yelling from Camille.

That's when I noticed the dogs had jumped the fence to the next property, where the abandoned cottage was nestled in the wooded area. I watched as Camille climbed the old wooden fence that'd seen much better days. The dogs were running up to the cottage, and Camille was running after them.

The door of the cottage must've been slightly opened because the dogs disappeared inside. Knowing Camille wasn't paying a bit of attention to me, I quickly ran to the fence line to get a closer look to see if she'd gotten the dogs after I noticed she'd gone inside the cottage.

With my back against one of the trees, I slowly peeked around and tried not to scream after I watched the two dogs walk out of the cabin with Camille.

A shotgun in her hand.

CHAPTER 11

"Oh my gosh, oh my gosh" were my exact words as I slinked down in a hurried walk back to my car, worried Camille was going to see me and use the gun on me this time.

My hands were shaking and my heartbeat thundered in my veins as I tried to put the keys into the ignition. They dropped onto the floorboard. I reached down without looking as I kept my eyes peeled on the corner of the house in case Camille came around the corner, and after a couple more stabs of putting the key into the car's ignition, I did it.

My brain didn't register the next steps, and when I realized it, I was halfway to Linden Falls before I got some wits about me. I glanced in the rearview mirror to make sure no one—namely Camille—was following me, and when I didn't see anyone, I pulled to the side of the road.

I reached to my console, and with a much steadier hand, I got my phone. I thumbed through my contacts until I found Hector's number and hit the green button.

"This is Hector," he answered.

"Hector, it's Cheryl Paisley." My voice shook even though I tried to keep it steady. "I know I might be wrong, but I subscribe to the 'see something, say something' philosophy, and well, I just saw Darlene Turner's daughter with a shotgun."

"Slow down. Are you saying you think you saw the murder weapon?" he asked.

"I'm saying I saw a shotgun in someone's hands who I think is very capable of having a good motive to have killed Zeke Turner." I felt so much safer telling him. My breathing got a little easier, and my nerves started to calm. "You aren't going to like this, but I have reason to believe Camille killed her stepfather over his excessive spending of her mother's funds and lifestyle change she was about to have due to the fact Zeke and Darlene were planning on moving to Middlesboro."

"And you know this how?" he questioned.

I spent the next five minutes telling him fairly quickly how I'd gotten the news, and I realized I'd dropped the file of the property Skye had given me next to the tree I was hiding behind. There was no way I was going back there to get it.

"And where are you going now?" he asked.

"I'm going back to my shop to close it so I can go home until I hear from you." I wasn't going to feel completely safe until Hector went to check out the shotgun.

"I'm going to head on over to Zeke's house and check out what you're saying. Please stop snooping around. If I have to ask you again, I'm going to have to charge you with tampering with evidence." Hector didn't act like he was appreciative of the information I'd given him, but I knew he was because he got off the phone fast.

A little calmer and clearer headed, I pulled the car back on the road, and when I got to the Stitchin' Post, I was much better. Especially after seeing Vance inside talking to a customer about knitting needles when I opened the door.

I flipped the sign on the door to Closed on my way inside and walked behind the counter, where I tossed my bag on the floor.

While Vance finished up with the customer, I walked into the back of the classroom to see if anyone was in there so I could tell them I was closing early. No one was there, and when I walked back into the shop, the customer was gone too.

"What's up?" Vance looked at me funny.

"Nothing." I didn't want to bother him with anything until I knew for sure what Hector was going to find out. No sense in spreading gossip. "I'm tired, and I wasn't able to get any vegetables from Darlene because she wasn't home, so I thought why not close up and go home to start our special dinner."

"You're amazing." He walked up to me and ran his fingers down my cheek. His hand landed on the small of my back, pulling me to him. "I was sitting here today watching the customers, looking around at what you've created. You're special, Cheryl."

His lips touched mine, and all the stress melted away.

"Really?" Sharon had let herself into the shop without us even hearing her. "No wonder the sign says Closed."

"Hey, Sharon." Vance smiled. "How's Truman?"

"Fantastic," she squealed with glee. "He and I had lunch today."

"Cheryl and I are having dinner at her cabin tonight." He looked at me. "Why don't you two join us?"

"That's a great idea." I couldn't be happier Vance invited them. I'd always wanted to be one of those couples who was friends with another couple where they did things together.

"I'll call him." She reached into her purse to get her phone and walked to the back of the shop to get some privacy.

"You close up here. I'll go finish up at the office, and I'll get the groceries on my way over to your cabin." Vance was really too much to be true.

"Are you sure?" I questioned. "I can close up and go get groceries."

"No. You have a few more boxes of yarn to put out and refill the stock I sold today." He grinned so big. "I think I'm a pretty good yarn salesman."

"You are indeed." I gave him another hug, and this time I initiated the kiss.

"Seriously. Truman and I aren't coming if you're going to kiss all night." She clutched her phone close to her heart.

"That means you're coming?" My eyes lit up.

"Yes." She bounced over with a huge smile on her face.

"That settles it." Vance laid a gentle hand on my arm. "I'm going to go to the office and grab the groceries on my way out to your cabin."

As soon as Vance walked out the door, Cheryl and I squealed with delight.

"This is everything we've always talked about," I told Sharon.

"I know! We will be in each other's weddings too!" Sharon was putting the cart before the horse, but I didn't correct her because this was going to be wonderful. "I was going to knit, but it looks like you're closing."

"I am because I need to get some of the new stock out." I would tell her later why I was really closing due to the fact I was exhausted and a bit scared of being here alone. There wasn't any reason to get her all excited with gossip. Waiting on information from Hector was the best thing to do instead of getting a rumor ahead of the facts.

"You can go knit. It'll take me an hour to get the stock out." I watched her walk behind the counter and grab her knitting bag she left there like most of the Linden Falls Knitters did. "Then you can just ride with me to my house, and Truman can take you home later."

"That sounds like a perfect plan." She walked back into the classroom.

Vance had stacked the few boxes next to the counter, making it easier for me to open them and put the merchandise out in the shop.

In order to get my mind off Zeke and the shotgun I'd seen in Camille's hands, I flipped on the radio to drown out my thoughts.

"I'm sorry, we are closed." I had forgotten to lock the shop door after Vance had left. I turned around, and it was Darlene with a couple of plastic grocery sacks.

"No problem. Camille told me you stopped by to get some vegetables." She lifted her hands. "I brought you some."

"Thank you so much." I gulped, wondering what had happened with

Hector. "How much do I owe?" I walked behind the counter and grabbed my knitting bag so I could retrieve my wallet.

"Nothing. I'm so grateful to have met you and your looking after me yesterday and today by coming by the house." She walked over and put the two bags filled with vegetables on the counter.

"No. I want to pay. We are small business owners." I noticed the file was stuck in one of the grocery bags. "I guess you found this."

"Hector did." She took it out and set it on the counter. "I'm afraid the realtor who you talked to is probably Zeke's killer. When Camille ran to get the dogs, she found the gun inside. She called Hector right after you did and told him she found it in there."

"Gosh. When I talked to Skye, I never got the impression she would do such a thing." I didn't want to upset Darlene more than she looked. She picked up my knitting needles to busy herself while I looked through the vegetables. "Not that I'm an expert because I think everyone is good. I have to say I'm sorry. Initially, I thought Camille had killed Zeke, and that's why I called Hector."

Darlene gave a slight smile, tears in her eyes.

"I'm so sorry." I hurried around the counter and wrapped my arms around her to offer a little comfort. "I do hope you join the Linden Falls Knitters."

"Mom! No!" The door of the shop flung open, causing me to look at Camille standing in the doorway with Hector next to her.

Out of the corner of my eye I saw Darlene's hand lifted in the air with my knitting needle pointed at my neck.

Out of nowhere and so fast I wasn't able to move, Sharon leapt across the display table full of the yarn I'd just taken out of the boxes, tackling Darlene to the floor.

Hector pushed his way into the shop and pulled Sharon off Darlene, slapping handcuffs on Darlene's wrists.

"Darlene Turner, I'm placing you under arrest for the murder of Zeke Turner." Hector had Darlene on her feet and walking her out the door of the Stitchin' Post as he recited her rights. Camille followed closely behind them.

"Oh my gosh." I heaved in and out as I tried to get my breath. "Thank you." I put my hand on my chest and looked at Sharon.

"I wasn't about to let anyone ruin our chances of being in each other's weddings. It took us years to make our wishes come true," Sharon joked just before a police officer came in to get our statements.

CHAPTER 12

"You mean you found out all of this information in the past few days?" Truman had made himself comfortable on one of the outdoor couches on my back patio.

Sharon walked around and refilled our wineglasses before she sat down next to him.

"Yes. At first I thought someone had set me up by replacing my wish, but from what the police officer who took my statement said, Camille had put the wish there." I looked at them and Vance. Vance put a hand on my thigh, squeezing it a little to show me he was supporting me to continue. "Camille had a feeling her mom had killed Zeke. She told Hector when he came to their house after I called about seeing her with the shotgun. She said her mom had gone out the night Zeke had gone to meet his friends for a game or two of poker at the Moose Lodge. When her mom came home a few hours later, Camille noticed mud on her shoes."

I looked down into my wineglass. A sadness draped over me like the blanket I'd knitted and laid on the back of the outdoor couch. I put my other hand on Tilly, who was curled up next to me. She liked to go outside, and I let her as long as she had her cat leash on.

I continued, "Camille didn't question anything, but when the dogs ran off to the cottage next door and she found the shotgun in there, she also noticed the shoeprints in the mud walking up to the cottage looked like they fit the muddy shoes Darlene had on that night."

"All of that running around you did, and all this time it was Darlene." Vance moved his hand from my leg to lay it around my shoulder. "Thank you, Sharon, for attacking Darlene."

"I heard the bell over the shop ding, and when I heard voices, I peeked out the classroom door. When I saw it was Darlene, I kept my ear to the door to see what she wanted. I've known Cheryl a long time, and she always sees the good in everyone." Sharon tsked. "Not me. I saw a little crazy in Darlene's eyes when Cheryl took the file out of the grocery bag."

"Did Camille ever say why her mom killed Zeke?" Truman asked.

"The officer said Darlene and Zeke fought a lot about money. He decided to purchase the land even knowing Darlene didn't want to do it. She'd told him to get a different job, but he wouldn't. He also told her she was going to have to get a job and kick Camille out of the house, or Camille was going to have to start paying them rent." I shook my head. "It was a lifestyle change Darlene didn't want, and he'd already gone through a lot of their money. According to the officer, Zeke had gotten a call on the Moose Lodge's phone from Darlene. None of them thought anything of it since it was his wife, but she was careful not to call on his phone so the police could trace it. He left the Moose and went to meet Darlene at the falls where she asked him to come."

I looked at all three of them with their jaws dropped.

"Camille told Hector her suspicions and said her mom just left with some vegetables and the file. She said she wasn't sure but believed her mom was going to come to the Stitchin' Post." I paused at the real possibility that if not for Camille and Sharon, I might not be alive. "I think when I told her I had talked to Skye and didn't buy Skye had killed Zeke that it flipped a switch, and that's when she grabbed my knitting needle to try to kill me."

"I'm no expert, but I think you need to hang up your sleuthing skills to unravel a mystery and stick with unraveling yarn." Truman's words hit home.

"Don't worry." I lifted my glass of wine. "My snooping days are over, and I'm only going to watch those shows, not be featured in one."

I glanced around with a grateful heart to be alive and surrounded by three good friends.

FROM TONYA

When I was asked to join the amazing authors of the Wishing Tree Series, I did question whether or not they knew I killed people...in fiction of course.

You see, the town is so amazing, full of friendships, love and how on earth were they going to feel about a little shake up in Linden Falls.

Luckily they said yes they'd love a shake up and well-here we are.

I truly hope you enjoyed Wishful Witness. I had a lot of fun getting to know the characters, shops, and town of Linden Falls.

I'm not going to say it wasn't hard writing in a shared world but even harder to write about the state of Vermont when I've never been there.

My heart lives and longs for the hollers in Kentucky where I reside in the deep woods, secluded from humans but live among trees and the creatures who reside there.

Wishful Witness, though about a murder mystery, is filled with friends who are always by our side and help us out in any situation-murder or just gossip.

You will find my cozy mysteries are charged with humor, friendship, family and life in small southern towns with quirky characters you'll be rooting for throughout the entire mystery.

If this sounds like something you'd love to continue reading, I invite you to check out all of books.

I hope you enjoyed WISHFUL WITNESS!

If so, please leave a review on Amazon, Goodreads, or Bookbub now. Reviews are so appreciated, they can be long, short, or just a star rating. Thank you!

Join my Cozy Mystery Club on Patreon!

Get exclusive-for-members-only activities, downloads, and more! Join today and get all my books!

About Tonya

Tonya has written over 100 novels, all of which have graced numerous bestseller lists, including the USA Today. *Best known for stories charged with emotion and humor and filled with flawed characters, her novels have garnered reader praise and glowing critical reviews. She lives with her husband and a very spoiled rescue cat named Ro. Tonya grew up in the small southern Kentucky town of Nicholasville. Now that her four boys are grown men, Tonya writes full-time in her camper she calls her SHAMPER (she-camper).*

Learn more about her be sure to check out her website tonyakappes.com. Find her on Facebook, Twitter, BookBub, and Instagram

Sign up to receive her newsletter, where you'll get free books, exclusive bonus content, and news of her releases and sales.

If you liked this book, please take a few minutes to leave a review now! Authors (Tonya included) really appreciate this, and it helps draw more readers to books they might like. Thanks!

Cover artist: Mariah Sinclair: The Cover Vault

Made in United States
Orlando, FL
05 February 2023

29486499R00055